Marcus

or, The Boy-Tamer

Walter Aimwell

Alpha Editions

This edition published in 2022

ISBN : 9789356786738

Design and Setting By
Alpha Editions
www.alphaedis.com
Email - info@alphaedis.com

Contents

PREFACE.

A LEADING aim of this little volume is to point out to elder brothers and sisters some of the ways in which they may exert a happy influence upon the younger members of the family. It also attempts, incidentally, to set forth the idea, that the best system of government for a child is that which trains him to govern himself. But while the author hopes his pages will not be wholly unsuggestive to such parents and "children of a larger growth" as may honor them with a perusal, he trusts there will remain enough both of story and moral for his younger readers, for whom, after all, MARCUS and the other volumes of this series are especially intended.

CHAPTER I.

THE PAGES.

"THERE'S the stage, mother! It's coming round the Bend,—don't you hear it? Hark! how near it sounds! I shall see it in a minute. There it is, now! And there's somebody on the top with Mr. Peters;—yes, there are two or three persons. I'll bet Marcus and Oscar are there; don't you believe they are? I'd ride outside, if I were they; wouldn't you, mother?"

"You had better not be too jubilant, Ronald," calmly replied the lady addressed. "Have you forgotten how disappointed you were last night?"

"O, well, it isn't likely they will disappoint us again," replied the boy. "I *know* they will come, this time, just as well as I want to. See! that's Marcus himself—I know him by his straw hat, and his brown linen sack that he wore to keep the dust off his clothes. And that boy by the side of him is Cousin Oscar, isn't it? Look! isn't that Oscar, Aunt Fanny?"

Aunt Fanny looked towards the stage-coach, still nearly a quarter of a mile distant; but her eyes were not sharp enough to distinguish the countenance of any one upon it, and she could not relieve the impatient boy from his suspense.

"I wonder what he looks like, any way," resumed Ronald. "I can tell, just as soon as I see him, whether I shall like him or not. Why, I should think he was as big as Sam Hapley. He looks a little like him, too, from here, doesn't he, mother?"

"I can't tell; he is hardly within the range of my vision, yet," replied Mrs. Page.

"Now Marcus is pointing this way," continued Ronald. "I'll bet he sees me, and is telling Oscar who I am. Why, mother, can't you see them now? I can almost hear them talk."

"Yes, that is Marcus, and there is Oscar, too," said Aunt Fanny, after gazing a few moments at the approaching coach.

"Didn't I tell you so!" exclaimed Ronald, rubbing his hands with glee, and dancing on the green sward around the door. "Speak to them, Rover!" he added, calling to a handsome spaniel that lay in the middle of the road, beneath the shade of a tree.

The dog sprang to meet the stage-coach, which was now within a few rods of the house; and, recognizing his master, he frisked around the horses, and manifested his satisfaction by a variety of significant signs.

Mr. Peters, the driver, reined up his horses at the farm house, and a young man, about eighteen years of age, jumped off, followed by a lad some three years younger. The first of these was Marcus Page, and this was his home, from which he had been absent about ten days, on a visit to Boston, and other places in Massachusetts. The other passenger was his cousin, Oscar Prestor, whose parents resided in Boston, but who had come to live with the family for a season. He appeared a little embarrassed, as he extended his hand to his two aunts, Mrs. Page, and her maiden sister, Miss Lee; but the cordial welcome which they extended to him, instantly put him at his ease. Meanwhile, little Ronald was gazing earnestly at the new-comer, evidently settling in his mind the important question which was to be decided at first sight, when Marcus said—

"Here, Oscar, let me make you acquainted with Master Ronald, my *protégé*. Ronald, this is Cousin Oscar. You will soon be good friends, if I am not greatly mistaken."

The boys shook hands, and then Ronald, proffering his services, helped Oscar to carry his trunk into the house. By the time the travellers had removed the dust from their persons and clothing, supper was ready, and the family sat down to the table. Much of the conversation, during the meal, was addressed to Oscar, and many inquiries were made concerning his parents, sisters, and brothers. He sustained his part with the ease and freedom of one who is accustomed to society, his first shyness having quite disappeared. Ronald watched him with much interest, and seemed still in doubt whether to like him or not. After tea, when Oscar had gone out with Marcus to the barn, Miss Lee, remembering Ronald's remark, inquired—

"Well, Ronald, what do you think of Oscar?"

"I think he feels pretty smart; and I never saw a city chap but what did," replied Ronald.

"Why, what makes you think so?" inquired Miss Lee.

"I don't know—I can't tell," said the boy, hesitatingly.

"But if you do really think so, you ought to be able to give a reason for it," added Miss Lee.

"Well," continued Ronald, "I suppose it's because he speaks up so smart, and eats so genteelly, and wears such nice clothes, and—and is so good-looking," he added, laughing at the idea.

"I think you are mistaken in him," replied Miss Lee. "His dress is such as boys in the city, of his age and class, usually wear; and his manners are those of a boy who is familiar with good society. Perhaps he is a trifle too forward, for one of his age,—I think a little bashfulness becomes a boy, sometimes;

but I never saw anything like pride in him. He has been about the world a good deal, for one so young, and that, I suppose, has worn off his bashfulness."

"Then I guess I shall like him, if he isn't proud," said Ronald, and away he ran, to join Marcus and Oscar, who were taking a general survey of the farm.

Mrs. Page's farm is situated in one of the pleasant mountain towns in Vermont, which, if it does not bear the name of Highburg on the map, will not, we trust, resent the act, if we venture to give it that designation, in this volume. It is located at the foot and on the sides of the Green Mountains, and within sight of one of their highest peaks, the Camel's Hump. Mr. Page was a sea captain, who, thinking it more pleasant to plough the land than the wave, purchased this farm in his native State, intending to make it his residence. When the new house and barns were completed, and the farm stocked with herds and flocks, and everything ready for occupancy, Capt. Page found that his money was all spent. Not having confidence enough in his agricultural skill to enter upon his new sphere of life without something in hand for an emergency, he determined to make one more voyage before he abandoned the sea. So he engaged a man to manage the farm during his absence, and, removing Mrs. Page and Marcus to their new home, he sailed on a whaling cruise, expecting to be gone about three years. It proved his last voyage in a sadder sense than he intended, for he never returned from it. Three, five, ten years passed away, but the missing ship was never heard from, and the owner of the farm never came back to enjoy the pleasant home he had prepared for himself. Mr. Burr, whom Capt. Page employed to oversee the farm, had managed its out-door affairs during all this period, although Marcus, within a few years, had taken a good share of the burden upon himself. During the winter months, indeed, Marcus now undertook the whole management of the farm. At this time the stock consisted of two horses, six or eight head of cattle, about seventy-five sheep, and a quantity of poultry.

When Oscar returned to the house, he found a boy and girl seated at the supper table, who were introduced to them as Katharine and Otis Sedgwick. They were brother and sister, and were pupils of the village academy, a mile or more distant. Katharine was about fourteen years old, and Otis some two years younger. They boarded at Mrs. Page's, and, with the persons already named, constituted the entire family.

Ronald, who called Mrs. Page mother, was a boy about twelve years old, whom she had undertaken to bring up. His parents were French Canadians, who had emigrated to the vicinity of Highburg, where they both died within a short time, leaving the poor child without friends or money. He was then about eight years old. Some of the kind people of the town wished to prevent his becoming a pauper, and tried to find a home for him; but, although he was a bright and interesting child, he could not speak English very plain, and was, moreover, very strange and wild in his manners and appearance, so that no one was willing to take him. Pitying his friendless lot, Mrs. Page at length offered to keep him a few weeks, till other arrangements could be made in his behalf. A month sped by, and no door opened for the little orphan but that of the poor-house. Wild, ignorant, unused to restraints, full of mischief, incapable of speaking or understanding the language of the family, and, in fact, almost as uncivilized as an Indian child, Mrs. Page found the new care a burden too great, and concluded that she must give up her charge to the town authorities.

When Marcus heard of this decision, he felt very badly. There was something about the little stranger, and his pitiable condition, that won upon his heart. So he put in a plea with his mother and Aunt Fanny in his behalf, and by way of further inducement, volunteered his own assistance in educating and training the child! Such an offer, from a boy who had but just passed his fourteenth birth-day, might provoke a smile from some people, and very properly, too. But neither Mrs. Page nor her sister thought of laughing at the suggestion. Marcus was not only a good scholar and a good boy, but he was more manly and mature, both in mind and body, than many youth of his age. As Ronald was more than six years his junior, it seemed plausible that Marcus might assist very much in making a man of him, and thus relieve his mother of a portion of the care. It was decided to try the experiment, and the result was so successful, that Mr. Upton, the principal of the academy, gave Marcus the title of "The Boy-Tamer." The boys soon became greatly attached to each other, and Marcus, by his example, influence and teachings, assisted very much in reclaiming the little savage. After a year or two, he was able to take upon himself almost the entire management of Ronald, directing his studies, imposing upon him his daily tasks about the farm, and generally exercising over him the authority and discipline of a father. Ronald, indeed, used sometimes to speak of him sportively as his "adopted father," and no doubt he seemed somewhat like a parent to the fatherless boy. His name, originally, was Ronald Doucette; but his new friends had given him their own name of Page, retaining Doucette as a middle name.

"How do you think Oscar appears, mother?" inquired Marcus, as soon as the withdrawal of the young folks to their bed-rooms left him alone with his mother and aunt.

"Very well," replied Mrs. Page. "He is a boy that can make a good appearance, if he chooses to. How does he seem pleased with his new home?"

"He doesn't say much about it," replied Marcus. "But he said, before we left Boston, that he was determined to be contented, whether or no. He is glad enough to come here, and I think he means to behave well. I told him this was probably his last chance, and that if he did not do well here, he would have to go back to the Reform School, and serve his full sentence out. But I don't think we shall have much trouble with him. He has behaved well in the institution, and he says he is determined to reform."

"And yet I am afraid he will find more difficulties in the way than he imagines," interposed Mrs. Page.

"But the difficulties here are nothing to what they would be in the city," added Marcus. "Nobody need know anything about his past life, here, and besides, he will be out of the way of his old associates and temptations."

"I think we ought to be very careful," said Aunt Fanny, "never to say anything about his past bad conduct, even to him. Nothing would discourage him so much as to have it known here that he had been a bad boy."

"I told him," replied Marcus, "that nobody here but we three knew anything about that,—not even Ronald; and I promised that it should be kept a secret, so long as he behaved well. He seemed very glad to hear it."

"He certainly has a favorable opportunity to make a new start in life, and I hope he will improve it," said Mrs. Page.

"We shall have to take a little time to study his character, before we can tell exactly how to manage him," continued Marcus. "I found out everything I could about him from his mother, and I think I begin to understand his disposition. The great lesson he has got to learn, is, to govern himself. Now that he has found, by experience, that if he does not put himself under restraint, others will do it for him, I think he is in a good state to learn this lesson."

The subject of these remarks was at this time between fifteen and sixteen years of age. He had been a headstrong, wayward boy, and had given his parents much pain. At one time, they sent him to live with an uncle in the village of Brookdale, in Maine, for the purpose of getting him away from his evil associates; but while there, he set fire to a large quantity of cut wood, which was destroyed, and was in consequence sent to jail, from which he was released only on his father's promise to remove him from the State. He was then sent on a short voyage to sea, but came back worse than before. His next downward step was to join a band of juvenile thieves; but his course was shortly afterward checked by his arrest, trial, and sentence to the Reform School during his minority,—that is, until he should be twenty-one years old. After he had remained in this institution about four months, his conduct having been good, and Mrs. Page, at the solicitation of Marcus, having offered to receive him into her family and endeavor to reform him, he was released by the officers, and given over to the care of his aunt and cousin; and his appearance in Highburg, at this time, was in accordance with this arrangement.[1]

> 1. The character and career of Oscar are more fully set forth in the first two volumes of this series, namely, "Oscar," and "Clinton."

CHAPTER II.

THE NEW-COMER.

THE new-comer, Oscar, was very naturally the recipient of much attention, for a few days after his arrival. The advent of such a big boy in the family was an event of no trifling importance, in the eyes of the younger members of the household. Was he not a real Boston boy, and had he not seen so much of city life that, in his own language, he was sick of it? Had he not also resided for months together in two or three other towns, far away from his home? And, most strange of all, had he not actually made a voyage to the West Indies, in the capacity of sailor-boy? So, at least, it was currently reported, and so they all believed; and surely a boy who had seen so much of the world must be something of a hero, they reasoned. Meanwhile, the older members of the family were quietly watching their new charge, studying his disposition, gaining insight into the secret springs of his character, and taking the measure of his mental acquirements and capacities.

Oscar was expecting to attend the academy, during the coming winter; but as it was now well advanced in the autumn term, he was to study at home until the new term commenced, about two months from this time, it being now the latter part of September. Marcus had graduated at this academy, a year previous, and had been invited to serve as assistant teacher, the coming winter.

"What shall *I* do?" inquired Oscar, the morning after his arrival, as he perceived that all the family were busily at work.

"You need not do anything, just yet," replied his aunt. "You can look on and see us work, through the rest of this week, or amuse yourself in any way you please. By next Monday we will find something for you to do, and you can commence your studies, too, at the same time."

The few days of leisure thus granted to Oscar did not hang very heavily upon his hands. He found many things to interest and amuse him, about the farm. The greatest novelty to him, however, were the sheep, for he had never before lived where these pretty creatures formed a part of the farm stock. The pasture where they were kept became at once an attractive place, and it must be confessed that the groups of sheep and lambs, quietly nibbling the grass, or reclining at their ease in the beams of the morning sun, formed as beautiful a scene as could be found upon the farm. The cattle, horses, pigs and poultry, the capacious barns, with the deep and lofty hay-mows, the dairy, granary, tool-house and wood-house,—these, also, though more familiar objects to Oscar, were not without their attractions for him; while he found a still further source of amusement in accompanying Marcus and Ronald, as they went about their daily duties on the farm.

Marcus was a little sorry to notice that Oscar did not appear to find idleness very irksome, nor to feel much anxiety about making himself useful. He seemed to think he had received a full discharge from labor for the rest of the week, and gave himself no more concern about it than though he was merely a boarder, like Katie and Otis, with whom he spent a good portion of his time. There were many little things in which his assistance, cheerfully offered, would have been accepted with pleasure; but we are sorry to say that these evidences of a "willing mind" were entirely wanting.

And yet Oscar went to Highburg with the determination of breaking up his old habits of idleness, and the terms upon which he was received into the family, had been arranged with this end in view. He was to remain here not less than two years. His father insisted upon paying for his board, clothing and schooling, during his residence here; but as one great object of the plan was to teach him to be industrious and useful, it was stipulated that he should do his share of the work on the farm, at all seasons of the year. It was further agreed that a fair sum should be allowed him for his services, to be paid to his father at the end of each year. If Oscar's conduct was satisfactory, this amount was to be paid over to him, when he reached the age of twenty-one. He thus had a real inducement to labor, in addition to the earnest entreaties of his parents; and lest both of these motives should prove insufficient, Marcus and his mother were authorized, as a last resort, to *enforce* the fulfilment of Oscar's part of the contract, by any means they saw fit to employ. His parents well knew that he could not be effectually reformed, until he had acquired habits of industry.

Nothing more was said to Oscar about work, until Saturday afternoon, when Marcus, finding the boys engaged in pitching jack-knives on the barn floor, accosted his cousin as follows:

"I suppose, Oscar, that you begin to feel as though you would like something to do?"

"Why, yes, I am almost tired of doing nothing," replied Oscar, shutting up his knife, and putting it in his pocket.

"Well, I can tell you something about your work and studies, now, if you wish," continued Marcus. "A good deal of your work, for awhile, will consist of odd jobs, which I cannot tell you about until they come along. For the present you must be ready for anything, in an emergency; we will be able, by and by, to systematize the work a little better, so that you needn't rob Ronald or me of our shares."

"No danger of that, I guess!" said Oscar, with a laugh.

"I don't know about that," continued Marcus. "We don't have a very great amount of out-door work in the fall and winter, and with three pairs of hands to divide it amongst, I'm afraid we may not all get our share, if we don't have an understanding about it. There's one department, however, that you shall have the sole charge of. Come this way."

He led the way to the wood-house, followed by the boys, and added:—

"There, Oscar, you shall be lord of the woodshed; and if any body meddles with the saw, axe, chips, or wood-pile, without your leave, just let me know it. Only you must understand that if I should want to chop a stick occasionally, by way of exercise, I shall have the liberty to do it."

"Oh yes, I'll agree to that," replied Oscar.

"And I too—I like to split wood once in a while," interposed Otis.

"And so do I," added Ronald.

"No, no, boys, you are not to touch anything here without Oscar's leave," said Marcus. "He is to be captain here, so you had better stand round. You see, Oscar, there is a large pile ready for use, now. My rule is, to saw and split a little more every week than we use, so as to have a good supply ahead, when cold weather sets in. I think you had better keep on in the same way, and make it a business, every day, or at least every other day, to add a little to the pile. It will also be a part of your work to see that a supply of wood is carried into the house every day."

"I'll help carry the wood in," said Ronald.

"But I told you not to interfere with his business," replied Marcus.

"Well, if he doesn't like it, then I wont do it," rejoined Ronald, laughing.

"As to the other work," resumed Marcus, "I shall want you to help cut up the hay, for one thing."

"I know how to do that," said Oscar.

"There will be a good deal of hay to cut, by and by, when the horses, cattle and sheep are all put up in the barn. And roots, too—we shall soon begin to feed them out, and they will have to be cut."

"I know how to do that, too," added Oscar.

"You can help about feeding the animals, too. I think I shall let you have the whole care of the pigs, to begin with, after a day or two. You will find them very interesting pets—especially the old sow!" he added, with a laugh.

"I might feed the horses," suggested Oscar, whose fancy for hogs was not very largely developed.

"So you can, and I want you to learn to bed them, and clean them out, and rub them down, too."

"I know how to do all that—I used to do it down to Brookdale, very often," replied Oscar.

"And I should like to have you help about milking; do you understand that?" inquired Marcus.

"I know a little about it, but I never liked it very well," replied Oscar, with some hesitation.

"O, well, I dare say you will like it better after you get used to it," said Marcus. "But if you shouldn't, it wont make much difference. We all have to do some jobs that are not so pleasant as others."

"I *like* to milk—only it tires my wrists," said Ronald. "I can milk one cow, all alone, but Marcus wont let me, very often."

"Next week," continued Marcus, "we must gather our apples, and you can help us about that. Then there will be the carrots, beets, turnips and cabbages to get in, the seed-corn to harvest, corn to husk, snow to shovel, wood to haul, and various other jobs to do, through the winter. Do you think you can do your share of all this?"

"I'll try to," replied Oscar.

"Then there are your studies to be attended to," resumed Marcus. "I shall make out a list of them, for each day in the week, while you study at home. And you must have some time for play, in addition to all the rest, for 'all work and no play makes Jack a dull boy.' The first thing, every day, will be to attend to your regular morning's work. Then, if there are any errands or extra jobs to be done, they will come next in order. After that, you will get your lessons, and then will come the play-time."

"How much time will he have for play?" inquired Otis.

"That will depend very much upon his diligence in doing his work and getting his lessons," replied Marcus.

"I shan't want much play-time," said Oscar, with a significant glance towards the couple of twelve-year-old urchins, who were evidently counting upon his companionship in their sports.

"So much the better," replied Marcus with perfect indifference, although, in his mind, he had some doubts about the last assertion.

Marcus had previously examined Oscar in his studies, and, in the course of the afternoon, he gave him lessons for the coming Monday, and also handed him a written list of studies for each day in the week. The list is as follows:—

ORDER OF STUDIES FOR OSCAR PRESTON.

ON MONDAY.

Writing,

Grammar,

Arithmetic.

ON TUESDAY.

Grammar,

Geography,

Arithmetic.

ON WEDNESDAY.

Writing,

Grammar.

ON THURSDAY.

Writing,

Geography,

Grammar.

ON FRIDAY.

Geography,

Arithmetic,

Writing.

ON SATURDAY.

Arithmetic,

Composition.

Reading, Spelling and Defining, daily.

CHAPTER III.

A BOY'S INFLUENCE.

"YOU silly boys! what are you doing?" exclaimed Kate, one afternoon, as she found her brother and Ronald seated on a log behind the barn, busily engaged in pricking Indian ink into their hands, with needles.

"You go away; we don't want you here," replied Otis, with rudeness, still pricking away with his needle, while the red and blue—the blood and ink—mingled and covered the spot upon which he was at work.

"There! it hurts, I know it does," said Kate, as her brother contracted his brows, and drew in his breath. "What ninnies you are to torture yourselves in that way, just for the sake of having some nasty ink pricked into your skin, where you never can get it out again!"

"I don't believe it hurts any more than having your ears bored; do you, Otis?" observed Ronald, remembering that Kate had lately submitted to the last-named operation.

"No; and 'tisn't any more foolish, either," replied Otis.

"Why, how absurd!" exclaimed Kate. "Ladies have to get their ears bored, to wear ear-rings, and besides, it doesn't hurt hardly any to bore them. I'm sure there's no comparison between the two things."

She did not stop to hear what answer might be made to this remark, and perhaps it was well that she did not.

"It *does* hurt, though!" exclaimed Otis, as soon as his sister was out of hearing. "O, doesn't it smart! Come, let's stop, now, and finish it some other time."

"No, I've got mine almost done, and I'm going to finish it now," replied Ronald, who was possessed of more endurance than his comrade.

Ronald persevered, and in a few minutes, wiping off the blood and ink, a rude resemblance to a star appeared in the red, inflamed flesh, between his thumb and forefinger. He seemed quite proud of the achievement, and going into the house, and extending his hand to Miss Lee, he accosted her with—

"See there, Aunt Fanny!"

"And see that, too!" said Otis, exhibiting his mark. "Mine isn't done yet, you see. It was so sore I had to stop, but I'm going to finish it some other time."

"What put it into your heads to do that?" inquired Miss Lee.

"O, nothing,—only the other boys do it," replied Ronald.

"Didn't you ever see Oscar's anchor?" inquired Otis.

"No, I didn't know he had an anchor," replied Miss Lee.

"He *has* got a real handsome anchor on his arm, pricked in with Indian ink," continued Otis.

"He made it when he was at sea,—and he has got a star like mine on his hand," said Ronald.

"I have noticed the star," said Miss Lee; "but what is the use of your marking yourselves in that way? What do you do it for?"

"Why, it looks handsome," replied Ronald, with some hesitation.

"I don't think so—those black marks look ugly, to me," replied Miss Lee; "besides, you never can wash them out."

"Why, that's the beauty of it, Aunt Fanny," replied Ronald, with one of his roguish looks. "There wouldn't be any fun in it if it washed out."

"Perhaps you will think differently, some time or other," said Miss Lee.

"But what hurt does it do?" inquired Otis.

"I don't know that it does any harm," replied Miss Lee; "but it always seemed to me like a heathenish practice. Did you know that the old pagans used to mark themselves in that way, in honor of their idols?"

"What, did they prick Indian ink into their hands, as we do?" inquired Ronald.

"Sometimes they pricked the marks in," replied Miss Lee, "and sometimes they burnt and cut them into the flesh. If a man devoted himself to Jupiter, he marked himself with a thunderbolt, on the palm of his hand, or his wrist, or neck, or upon some other part of his body. If he chose Mars for his god, then the mark was a helmet or spear. Soldiers and slaves used sometimes to be marked in the same way, to show to what commander, or to what master, they belonged. Some tribes of savages, at the present day, are very fond of such ornaments, and tattoo their faces all over, by pricking dyes into their skins. There are several allusions to this custom in the Bible, and the Jews were forbidden to practise it."

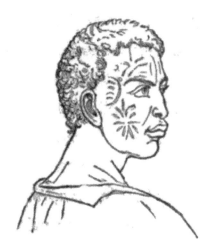

"It's wicked, then, to make such marks, isn't it?" inquired Otis.

"No," replied Miss Lee, "so long as you do not make them in honor of any false god, nor with any bad motive, there is no sin in the act. The worst that can be said about it is, that it is a foolish custom, and a relic of paganism and superstition."

"I'm going to see if I can't wash mine out, before it dries in," said Ronald, and he hurried off to the pump, followed by Otis.

For a few minutes the boys worked as hard to rub out their new ornaments as they had labored, a little while before, to imprint them upon their hands. But water, soap, and even sand, were all in vain. The stars shone as brightly at the end as at the beginning of the effort. While thus engaged, Oscar came along, and, on seeing what the boys were about, indulged in a hearty laugh.

"Why, you little fools!" he exclaimed, "what are you trying to wash the ink out for?"

"Because we don't want it in," replied Ronald.

"What did you prick it in for, then?" continued Oscar.

"Because we didn't know any better, then," said Ronald; "but Aunt Fanny says the heathen prick ink into their hands, and I don't want to be a heathen."

"Well, if that isn't a great idea!" exclaimed Oscar, relapsing into another hearty laugh. "I suppose you think I'm a heathen, then, don't you?" he continued. "Well, if I'm a heathen, I guess there are a good many others around full as bad. I never heard any body say there was any harm in pricking a little Indian ink into your hand, and I don't believe there is, if Aunt Fanny does say so."

"She didn't say there was any harm in it," replied Ronald. "She said she didn't like it, because it was doing as the heathen did."

"So we 'do as the heathen do' when we eat, but I shan't give up eating on that account," observed Oscar.

"Nor I, either," said Otis, who was very willing to be re-converted to the tattooing process. "I mean to finish my star—what's the use of trying to wash it out?"

"Star! do you call that thing a star?" inquired Oscar, with a look of contempt.

"But I haven't finished it," meekly interposed Otis.

"No, I shouldn't think you had," added Oscar. "It looks more like a spider than a star. If I couldn't make a better star than that with my eyes shut, I'd put my head under a bushel basket."

With this self-sufficient remark, Oscar walked off, and Ronald and Otis, having come to the conclusion that their stars were beyond the reach of soap and sand, also left the room. It happened that Mrs. Page and Miss Lee were sitting in an adjoining room, and overheard the conversation just related.

One afternoon, some time after this occurrence, as Oscar was sitting with his Aunt Fanny, in her chamber, studying his lessons, a boy of about his age came along, with a gun on his shoulder, and seeing Oscar at the open window, called him, in a low voice—

"Come, Oscar; want to go over to Prescott's?"

"No, I can't go; I've got my lessons to learn," replied Oscar.

"How long before you'll be done?" inquired the boy, whose name was Samuel Hapley, and who lived near by.

"It will take me nearly all the afternoon, I suppose," replied Oscar.

"Then I'm off," said the boy, resuming his course.

Oscar watched him somewhat wishfully for a minute or two, as he directed his course through the fields, and then turned to his books. Sam Hapley was the only boy near his own age in that part of the town; and it also happened that he was the only boy in Highburg he had been cautioned against. His aunts and Marcus knew that he could not well avoid forming an acquaintance with Sam, and they did not forbid this; but they earnestly advised Oscar to associate with him as little as possible, and to beware of his evil influence. Sam's father was intemperate. His mother was sickly, discouraged and disconsolate. The children, of whom Sam was the oldest, were neglected, their father being cross and severe with all of them except the youngest, and their mother always attempting to shield them from his displeasure, even when they had done wrong. The farm wore an air of thriftlessness, and, to crown their misfortunes, it was covered with mortgages.[2]

> 2. A mortgage is a pledge of property by a debtor to a creditor to secure a debt. For instance, a man who owns a farm wishes to borrow a thousand dollars, and to secure the lender from loss, he pledges his farm to him. The farm is then said to be mortgaged. The borrower cannot dispose of it, and the lender is, in effect, its real owner, to the amount of his claim, until that claim is paid. If it should not be paid when due, the lender, or mortgagee, as he is called, may sell the farm, after a certain time, and thus get his money back. When an intemperate man mortgages his property, there is little hope that he will ever redeem it.

"You got rid of him pretty easily, that time," said Miss Lee, as Sam passed along.

"I know it; but I shouldn't have gone if I had got my lessons," replied Oscar.

"It makes me real sad to see how that boy has changed, within ten years," continued Miss Lee.

"He was once a pretty, modest, gentle boy, and used to be quite a favorite of mine. Now, the coarse features of vice are settling upon his face, and he is said to be a very bad boy."

"He swears like everything," remarked Oscar.

"So I have heard," added Aunt Fanny.

"Henry swears some, too," continued Oscar, alluding to a brother of Sam, about thirteen years old.

"Ah, I am sorry to hear that," said his aunt. "But it isn't very strange, after all, with such an example before him. A boy of Sam's age exerts a great influence on his young brothers and sisters. The little children look up to the large ones with a sort of fear and respect, and copy their ways, and imitate their example, right or wrong. Did you ever think how much influence of this kind you may be exerting?"

"I don't know that I ever thought much about it," replied Oscar.

"Here are three children in the family," continued his aunt, "younger than you. The fact that you are older and have seen more of the world than they, while you are still a boy, gives you quite an influence over their minds. You can increase or diminish that influence, according to the manner in which you treat them; but you can't wholly divest yourself of it. You must exert an influence over them, good or ill, in spite of yourself, and when you are not thinking of it. I saw an illustration of this, a few days ago. Otis and Ronald noticed that you had a star pricked into your hand, and what did they do but prick stars into theirs, as soon as they could get the materials!"

"Oh yes, I noticed that," said Oscar, laughing.

"That was a trifling thing," resumed Aunt Fanny, "but it illustrates a great truth. It shows how you are watched, and copied, and it ought to put you on your guard. You can use this influence so as to assist us in training the children to good habits, or, if you choose, you can do just the opposite. You see there is quite a responsibility resting upon you. If they see that you are studious, industrious and faithful, they will feel an influence drawing them in the same direction; but if you exhibit any bad trait, it would not be strange if they should try to pattern after it."

"I never thought much about that before, but I mean to look out for it now," said Oscar.

Nothing was said to Oscar in relation to his unguarded remarks to the boys about tattooing, and he never knew that he was overheard by his aunt. That incident, however, gave the turn to the conversation on this occasion.

CHAPTER IV.

UP THE MOUNTAIN.

OSCAR, from the day of his arrival in Highburg, had expressed a desire to ascend some one of the lofty mountain peaks in the neighborhood; and Marcus had made a sort of half promise to get up a party, some fine autumn day, to visit the Camel's Hump, the highest eminence in that part of the State. On reflection, however, it was thought best to abandon this undertaking, on account of the distance of the mountain from Highburg, the difficulty of making the ascent, and the time that would be required for the expedition. But to compensate Oscar and the other young folks for the disappointment, it was determined, one Saturday afternoon, to make an excursion to a notable eminence called "Prescott's Peak," situated about two miles from Mrs. Page's.

The party consisted of Marcus, Oscar, Kate, Ronald, Otis, and Rover, the dog. They struck an air-line towards the mountain, through fields, meadows and woods, Rover strolling on ahead of the party, with an air of entire satisfaction.

"I'll bet Rover knows where we are going—don't you believe he does, Marcus?" inquired Oscar.

"I don't know, I almost think sometimes that he knows what we say," replied Marcus.

"He knows a good deal that we say, any way," remarked Otis. "You give him a bucket, and tell him to carry it out to the barn, and he'll do it just as well as anybody; and he'll lie down, or give you his paw, or speak, if you tell him to."

"One day, about a year ago," said Marcus, "when Aunt Fanny was packing her trunk, to go to Grandmother's, she told Rover she had got to leave him, and asked him if he didn't want to go, too; and upon that he jumped right into her trunk,—as much as to say, 'Yes, I want to go,—pack me in!' When Aunt Fanny came back from her journey, it seemed as if he would eat her up, he was so glad to see her. He never forgets anybody that he has once known. Last summer, I took him over to Montpelier with me, where he used to live; and although he hadn't been there for over two years, he remembered all his old friends, and went around and scratched at all the doors of the houses he used to visit when he lived there."

"And he's the neatest dog that I ever heard of,—he wont come into the house with dirty paws," added Kate.

"No," continued Marcus, "and once when we had our floors newly painted, and boards were laid to step upon, Rover understood the arrangement as well as we did, and was careful to walk upon the boards until the paint was dry."

"We had a strange dog come to our house last winter, that knew something," said Otis. "He *knocked* at the door, just as well as a man could have done it. Mother went to see who had come, and she found nothing but a dog. As soon as he saw her, he began to cry like a baby, he was so cold and hungry. So she gave him some dinner, and let him warm himself, and then he went off, and we never saw him again. But he knocked at the door,—tap, tap, tap,—so you couldn't have told him from a man."

"I could tell a story that would beat that," said Oscar. "I knew a dog in Boston that would open any door that was fastened by a latch, without stopping to knock; and he'd shut it, too, if you told him to."

"I could tell a story that would beat all of yours," said Ronald. "It's about a dog that *unlocks* doors; and if he can't find the key, he will hunt up a piece of wire, and *pick the lock!*"

"Why, Ronald Page! how dare you tell such a lie?" exclaimed Kate, after the laugh that followed this sally had subsided.

"It wasn't a lie," replied Ronald. "I didn't say a dog ever did that—I said I could tell a *story* about a dog that did it, and so I can."

"It's a lie, for all that; I'll leave it to Marcus if it isn't," rejoined Kate.

"Not exactly a lie, although it looks something like it," observed Marcus. "Ronald could not have intended to deceive anybody, when he told such a tough story as that, and therefore it was not a falsehood. But"—

"A snake! a snake!" suddenly broke in Ronald, who was a little in advance of the others.

"O, kill it! do kill it!" cried Kate, running back a few steps from the scene of danger.

"No, I shan't—you said I lied, and now you want me to commit murder, do you?" retorted Ronald.

"Pooh! it's nothing but the cast-off skin of a snake," said Otis, lifting it upon a stick, and tossing it toward Kate, who dexterously dodged the missile.

"That was the skin of a black snake, wasn't it?" inquired Oscar.

"Yes," replied Ronald, "and a pretty large one, too."

"I saw a black snake all of six feet long, that summer I was down to Brookdale," said Oscar. "Jerry and I were on a high rock, and saw the snake in the field below us. He was coiled up, and was watching a squirrel that was a little way off. We got some stones, and pelted him, but I believe we didn't hit him, for we couldn't find anything of him."

"I killed a large black snake, all alone, down in our meadow, not more than a month ago," said Ronald.

"Is that one of your yarns, or do you expect us to believe it?" inquired Oscar.

"It's the truth, sir, I'll leave it to Marcus, if it isn't," replied Ronald.

"Hold on a minute," said Marcus, stopping by the side of a small, shallow pond they were passing; and, taking a stick, he began to stir up its muddy bottom.

"What in the world is he dabbling in that dirty water for?" inquired Kate.

"I guess he is hunting for frogs' eggs," said Ronald; "or, perhaps he's going to make some pollywog soup."

"Do you see, he is going to set the pond afire!" cried Kate, as Marcus drew some friction matches from his pocket.

Marcus continued his operations, without noticing the comments of his companions, and in a little while, he actually produced a faint yellow flame upon the surface of the water, to the astonishment of the company. He then explained to them that this was an experiment which he had learned while studying chemistry at the academy. When vegetable matter decays under water, a gas called light carburetted hydrogen is formed, which may be burned. On stirring up the bottom, the gas escapes, and rises to the top in bubbles, and may be collected in jars, or set on fire upon the surface of the water. This gas, he said, was the terrible "firedamp," which caused such tremendous explosions in coal mines, before Sir Humphrey Davy invented his safety lamp, to protect the miners from these disasters. He told them, also, that he had seen it stated in a newspaper that on one of our Western rivers, when the water was very low, the steamboats had to shut down their furnace doors for several miles, and allow no torches to be lighted at night, for fear of "setting the river on fire!" Frequently boats that did not use these precautions at this particular place, have found themselves engulfed in flames, greatly to the alarm of the passengers, and sometimes setting the steamers on fire. In some instances, the passengers have come very near leaping overboard, before the officers could convince them that there was no danger; an act that would be almost literally "jumping from the frying-pan into the fire."

The party now resumed their course, and after skirting a swamp, and threading their way thro' a tangled growth of young birches and pines, and breaking a path through the sharp, bristling stubble of a rye field, they reached the foot of the mountain. The eminence was clothed with that dress of unfading green from which this range takes its name,[3] being covered with spruce, fir, hemlock, and other evergreens, to the summit. They began the ascent by a narrow, steep and winding path, which, however, had the appearance of being much used.

> 3. The range was named *Verd Mont* by the early French settlers, which means in English, Green Mountain. When the people declared themselves a free and independent State, in 1777, they adopted the French name as that of their Commonwealth, contracting it by the omission of the *d*.

"I should think a good many people came up here, by the looks," remarked Oscar.

"Not many, except Gooden's folks," replied Marcus.

"Who is Gooden?" inquired Oscar.

"He is a strange fellow who lives up on the mountain," replied Marcus. "We shall come to his cabin pretty soon, and perhaps you will have a chance to see him."

"But what does he live up here for, away from everybody?—is he cracked?" inquired Oscar.

"He lives here because he prefers to keep out of the way of people, I suppose," replied Marcus.

"They say he used to steal, and got caught in a trap, once," said Kate.

"A regular *steal* trap, wasn't it?" inquired Ronald.

"That is the common report," added Marcus, not noticing Ronald's pun, "and I suppose it is true. The story is, that where he used to live, his neighbors found their grain going off faster than they thought it ought to, and one of them set a large bear trap, with steel springs and sharp teeth, to catch the thief. One morning soon after, he went out to the barn, and found Gooden fast in the trap. It caught him around the ankle, and they say he was laid up for several months with a sore leg. He is a little lame, now, from the effects of it. As soon as he could get away, he came and settled in this out-of-the-way place, and lives as much like a hermit as he can, with his family."

"O, has he got a family?" inquired Oscar.

"Yes, a wife and four children," replied Marcus.

"How does he support himself, now,—by stealing?" inquired Oscar.

"No," replied Marcus, "nobody suspects him of dishonesty, now—he is probably cured of that. He owns a cow, and raises corn and potatoes enough to support his family. He kills some game, which supplies him with meat. They get a little money by making maple sugar, and collecting spruce gum. But after all they are quite poor, and people often give them clothing, and other necessary articles. The children are growing up in ignorance, too,— they never go to school or church. They will stand a rather poor chance in the world, brought up in that way."

After toiling up the zigzag path awhile longer, the party came to an open, level space, and found themselves within a few rods of Gooden's cabin, a small, rude structure, built of rough logs, with a large chimney at one end, on the outside. Several children were playing around the house, and the father himself was just coming in from a hunting excursion up the mountain, with his gun on his shoulder, and his dog by his side. Seeing the party approaching, Mr. Gooden went into the house and shut the door. Marcus had often visited the family, on errands of kindness, but knowing the morose and suspicious disposition of the father, and his antipathy to company, he concluded not to stop at the cabin. Exchanging a few words with Jake and Sally, the two oldest children, who stood staring at the strangers, Marcus passed on, with his party, through a path still more intricate and difficult.

"You said something about spruce gum—what do they do with it?" inquired Oscar.

"They sell it," replied Marcus. "A man comes round here every summer, who makes it his business to collect spruce gum. He buys all the gum that is offered him, and he hires boys to gather it for him, paying them so much a pound. This gum is cleaned, and sent to the cities, where it brings a good price."

"Well, if everybody was like me, the spruce gum trade wouldn't be worth much," said Kate. "I don't see why anybody wants to chew the nasty stuff, especially a young lady. How it looks, to see your jaws going the whole time! There are some girls in the academy that always have their mouths full of gum. I think it's real disgusting."

"Chewing gum isn't quite so bad as chewing tobacco, but it is a foolish and disgusting habit, as you say," observed Marcus.

The party continued their ascent up the steep and slippery side of the mountain, occasionally halting a few minutes to take breath. Some of them began to question whether there was any top to it, as each turn of the zigzag path, which promised to land them at the summit, only revealed as they advanced a still higher point beyond. But at length the top, the very "tip-top," as the boys called it, was reached. Instead of a sharp, sky-scraping ridge, they found the summit to be a broad and nearly level plain, composed mostly of solid rock, and almost bare of vegetation. But what a view did it present! A dozen villages scattered among the valleys, with their nestling houses and white spires; the rich meadows of the Winooski and its tributaries, with their thrifty farms; the cattle and sheep "upon a thousand hills;" the dark and extensive patches of forest, in which the woodman's axe has never yet resounded; the chain of mountain sentinels, drawn up in lines, conspicuous among which were the Camel's Hump, and the distant Mansfield Mountain, with its "Nose," "Lips" and "Chin;" the broad and peaceful expanse of Lake Champlain, with a faint outline of the Adirondack Mountains looming up beyond;—such is a very imperfect sketch of the scene that for a long time engrossed the attention of the whole party.

After the party had rested themselves, and gazed at the extensive prospect as long as they wished, Oscar proposed to erect a monument on the summit that would be visible from their house, and would commemorate their ascent of the mountain. The proposal was readily agreed to by all, and they immediately set about gathering the necessary materials. All the movable stones on the summit were soon collected in a heap, but Marcus expressed a doubt whether there were enough to form a pile that would be visible below.

"If we only had an axe," said Oscar, "we could cut down a tree, and strip off all the branches but a few at the top; and then we could set the tree on the summit, and pile the stones about it to keep it in place."

"Has anybody got any string about him?" inquired Otis.

There was a general fumbling of pockets, and among a score of miscellaneous articles produced was a piece of old fishing-line belonging to Ronald.

"That's just the thing," said Otis. "Now we will find a tree that has blown down, and tie a lot of new branches to the top of it, and stick it up, as Oscar said."

This proposal was adopted. A tall, straight sapling was soon found, that had fallen before the furious winter blasts that play among the Peak. Its branches, now partially decayed, were broken off, and the trunk made as clean as possible, with the exception of the top. A quantity of evergreen boughs were then procured, and lashed to the top of the sapling by the fishing-line. The signal pole, with its heavy tuft, was now raised to its place by the united strength of the party, and the stones piled compactly around its bottom, until it seemed as firm as though rooted in the earth. Three cheers were given for the monument, and then, after a short resting-spell, the party began to descend.

With merry shouts and laughter they were bounding, sliding and tumbling down the steep side of the mountain, the boys sometimes far outstripping Kate and Marcus, and then pausing awhile, to see how their more moderate companions got along. In this way they had proceeded nearly a quarter of a mile from the summit, when Kate suddenly brought them to a stand by exclaiming—

"I declare! if I haven't left my veil on the top of the mountain! I took it off when we were looking at the scenery, because it was in my way, and I forgot to put it on again."

"That's just like you," said her brother; "you are always forgetting something."

"Never mind, I'll run back and get it—it wont take but a few minutes," said Oscar.

"No, let me go—I'm more used to it than Oscar is," exclaimed Ronald.

"I'd let her go herself—it would make her more careful next time," said Otis, in a low tone, which he did not intend Marcus should hear.

"Ronald is the nimblest, and he has been up the mountain before; so I think he had better go and get the veil, and we will wait for him till he gets back," said Marcus.

Ronald accordingly scrambled up the hill again, while the others seated themselves on the dry leaves beneath a noble pine.

"I don't see what girls want to wear veils for," said Otis, somewhat petulantly, after they were seated.

"It isn't necessary for you to know why they wear them, Master Otis," replied Kate, quite coolly.

"I have no objection to girls' wearing veils, if they choose to, but I don't like to see boys wear such things," said Marcus.

"Why, did you ever see boys wear veils?" inquired Otis, with surprise.

"I have seen boys that I thought acted as if they wore veils over their eyes," replied Marcus.

"How did they act?" inquired Otis, after a moment's pause.

"They acted as if they could not see things that were as plain as a pike-staff to other people," replied Marcus.

Otis seemed to be trying to interpret to himself this enigmatical language, but did not appear inclined to ask any more questions.

"For instance," added Marcus, after a brief pause, "when you see a boy rude or unkind towards his sister, when there is no provocation, you may conclude that he has a veil or something else over his eyes; for if he could see plainly how such conduct looks to other people's eyes, he would not indulge in it."

Otis apparently understood the point of the remark, and felt it, too; but he made no reply. In a few minutes a merry shout announced the approach of Ronald, and he soon appeared, with the lost veil fastened to his straw hat. He claimed the privilege of wearing it home, which Kate readily granted; but before the party came in sight of the log cabin, he concluded to surrender it to its owner.

Going down the mountain proved almost as difficult and exciting as climbing up, and many a slip and tumble happened to one and another, on the way. Sometimes a low branch across the path, bent from its place and then let loose by one, would bring up the boy behind with a whack that made him see stars. By one of these flying limbs Otis had his cap suddenly removed from his head, and whirled over a precipice, lodging in the top of a tall tree below. The disaster was followed by a prolonged and hearty shout from those who witnessed it, and the others hastened to the spot, to see what the matter was.

"I'll get it for you, Oty—I can climb that tree easy enough," exclaimed Ronald, as soon as he comprehended the extent of the mishap.

"No," said Marcus, with assumed gravity, "let him get his cap himself—it will make him more careful next time."

"I don't see what boys wear caps for; they are always losing them," remarked Kate, the fun in her eyes but half concealed.

"It wasn't my fault—I couldn't help it," replied Otis, with the utmost seriousness. "Ronald let the branch fly right into my face, and it took my cap off before I knew it was coming."

"Well, if Ronald is to blame, I think we shall have to send him after the cap," said Marcus.

They made their way, with some difficulty, to the spot where the tree stood. Ronald, being a more expert climber than any of the others, was entrusted with the job, and ascended the tree almost with the agility of a squirrel. He took with him a pole, and with its aid the cap was soon dislodged, and sent to the ground below.

No further incidents of importance befell the party, on their descent of the mountain. Mr. Gooden did not manifest himself to them, as they passed his cabin; and none of his family were visible. They reached their home, tired and hungry, in season to get a view of the signal they had raised, after the sun had sunk behind Prescott's Peak; and there the tall sapling stood, for a long time afterwards, reminding them of their pleasant tramp "up the mountain."

CHAPTER V.

THE BLOTTED WRITING-BOOK.

THERE were loud demonstrations of joy among the juvenile members of the household, one morning, when Marcus handed a letter to Kate, for Mr. Upton, the principal of the academy, and informed them that it contained his acceptance of the office of assistant teacher in that institution, for the winter term. The appointment had been offered him several weeks previous, and had been the subject of much consideration on the part of Marcus, and of no little interest, also, among the children, who were all anxious to have Marcus for a teacher, notwithstanding he repeatedly forewarned them, that if he should show them any particular favor as their instructor, it would only be by looking more sharply after them than he did after the other scholars.

"Three cheers for Master Page!" shouted Ronald, and they were given, with as much power as four noisy throats could command.

"You know me, Marcus,—you'll excuse me from writing compositions, wont you?" inquired Kate, when the noise had subsided.

"You know me, too, Marcus,—you wont make me speak pieces, will you?" said Otis.

"You know me, Master Page,—you wont make me do any thing, will you?" added Ronald, capping the climax.

"Yes, I know you, you young rogue, and if you don't walk straight you'll catch it!" said Marcus, in reply to the last speaker.

Ronald did not take the admonition much to heart; but concluded his demonstrations of delight by throwing his cap over an apple tree, turning two somersets, and crowing like a "rooster," whose clarion notes he could imitate with ludicrous fidelity. Then, leaping upon the back of Otis, who with Kate was just starting for school, he disappeared; but his voice was uppermost among the joyous shouts and laughter that came across the fields long after their departure.

Kate and Otis did not usually go home from school at noon, but carried their dinners with them, the distance being too great to walk. Ronald, however, generally dined at home, the district school, which he was now attending, being less than a mile distant from Mrs. Page's. In the course of the forenoon, before the hour of school dismission, as Marcus was at work throwing up muck from a meadow, he was surprised to see Ronald approaching, on the road leading to the house. "He must be sick," thought Marcus, as he noticed how slowly he walked, and how silent and dejected he appeared. What a change had come over the light-hearted boy, within two hours!

Ronald appeared to hesitate a moment, and then turned into the meadow, towards Marcus. As soon as he was within speaking distance, the latter inquired what the matter was. Ronald made no reply until he had reached the place where Marcus stood, and then he exclaimed:—

"I'm not going to *that* school any more—I've been licked for nothing, and I wont stand it!"

"And how came you home at this time of day?" inquired Marcus.

"I ran away from school," replied Ronald.

"Indeed!" said Marcus; "and will you please to explain why?"

"Mrs. Benham set out to lick me——"

"Begin at the beginning, and tell the whole story," interrupted Marcus. "What did she punish you for?"

"Why, you see she was real cross this morning," said Ronald; "I saw it as soon as she got there, and thought there'd be a squall before night. Well, I was studying my lesson, and she came along, and wanted to look at my writing-book. So I handed it to her, and she opened it, and found four or five great blots on the page I wrote yesterday afternoon. She looked real mad, and asked me what it meant, and I told her I didn't do it, and didn't know anything about it. Then she said I lied, and she'd whip me for blotting the book, and for lying, too. So she made me go out to the platform, and began to put on the ratan over my hands, just as hard as she could. See that," continued Ronald, showing to Marcus several red stripes on the palm of his hand. "I couldn't stand that, so I got the stick away from her, and ran off as fast as I could. I didn't blot the book, nor tell a lie, and I wont be whipped for nothing by Mrs. Benham, I know."

"Have you told me the truth, about this affair, and nothing but the truth?" inquired Marcus, fixing a steady gaze upon Ronald.

"Yes, sir, I've told the real truth, and nothing else," replied Ronald.

"Is it the whole truth?" inquired Marcus. "Have you not kept something back?"

"Why, I pulled the teacher over, when I got the stick away,—I believe I didn't tell you about that," replied Ronald, in a lower tone. "I didn't mean to do it, though. She was on the edge of the platform, and I was standing on the floor, and when I caught the ratan and jerked it away, she fell upon the floor, somehow, and then I ran off."

"How do you know that she was not injured by the fall?" inquired Marcus.

"O, it didn't hurt her, for she chased me out to the door, and shook her fist at me,—I turned around and saw her," replied Ronald.

"Well, you have got yourself into a pretty scrape," said Marcus, "and it's my opinion you have not seen the worst of it yet. According to your own story, you are liable to be arrested for assault and battery, and what's to be done, then?"

"I didn't assault her, nor batter her; she held on to the stick, and I just pulled her over, that was all," replied Ronald.

"You resisted your teacher, and pulled her upon the floor; and that is sufficient, I think, to constitute what the law terms assault and battery," said Marcus. "At any rate, I do not see but that you will have to go back and apologize to her, before the school, and then let her finish the flogging she intended to give you, if she chooses. I think that would be the easiest way to settle the difficulty. You had better go home and tell mother about it, and see what she says."

Ronald turned away with a sadder heart than ever. He revolted at the thought of a public apology and submission, and secretly determined that he would not yield to such a humiliation. He went home and told his story to Mrs. Page, who seemed much grieved and troubled by his conduct. She questioned him very closely about the blots on the writing-book, from which all the trouble sprang; but he protested that he knew nothing about them, with great apparent sincerity. Still, she remembered that Ronald was much addicted to lying, when he came to live with her; and though the habit had been broken up, by patient labor and often severe discipline, there was a lurking fear that he might possibly have relapsed, under a strong temptation.

When Marcus came in to dinner, Ronald's case was freely discussed, and the conclusion appeared to be unanimous that they could not sustain him in the course he had taken, even if he were innocent of the fault for which he was punished. It was argued that a school government must, of necessity, be a sort of absolute monarchy. The teacher, although responsible to the community, and more immediately to the committee, if it be a public school, is *not* accountable to his pupils. Among *them* he is king, and resistance to his authority is treason. He may sometimes seem unreasonable in his requirements, but his scholars are not the best judges of this. He may even sometimes punish the innocent, by mistake; but in such a case, it is better to submit to a little temporary pain and mortification, trusting in a future redress or reparation, rather than to defy or resist his authority in the presence of the school, thereby shaking the foundation of his government. So reasoned Mrs. Page, Aunt Fanny, and Marcus, and they thus reached the conclusion that

Ronald was guilty of a flagrant offence in school, and was liable to expulsion, if not prosecution.

In the afternoon, just before it was time to dismiss school, Marcus went to see the teacher, taking Ronald with him, who, by the way, was quite reluctant to go. Mrs. Benham received them politely, and after the school closed, Marcus told her Ronald had informed him that he had had a difficulty with her, and requested her to give him an account of the affair.

"Something more than a difficulty," replied the teacher; "it was a downright attack upon me, and I feel the effects of it yet. I never was abused in that way by a boy before. The way it commenced was this: I asked Ronald to let me look at his writing-book, and I found several large blots on the last page he wrote. I felt doubly provoked, because his was the neatest writing-book in the boys' department, and I wished it kept nice, for the committee to examine. When I called him to account for the blots, he answered, as children are apt to do in such a case, that he didn't know anything about them, and never saw them before. That was a very improbable story, and I felt almost sure, from his actions, that he was telling me a lie. So I told him I should be obliged to punish him if he attempted to deceive me. He answered, in an impudent tone, that 'he hadn't done anything, and wasn't going to be whipped for nothing.' I talked with him further about it, and tried to persuade him to tell the truth, but he grew more obstinate and saucy, and threatened that he would never come to school again if I punished him. I thought it was time then to take him in hand, so I began to punish him with the ratan; but before I had given him half a dozen blows, he caught hold of the stick, and in jerking it away from me, some how threw me down upon the floor. He then ran off and took my stick with him. I hurt my shoulder, in falling, and it is quite sore, now."

"You didn't tell me you were impudent, Ronald; why did you keep that back?" inquired Marcus.

"I didn't know that I was impudent," replied Ronald.

"You said I shouldn't punish you, and that you would never come to school again if I did; shouldn't you call that impudent, Marcus?" inquired the teacher.

"Yes, I call that impudent language, when addressed to a teacher," replied Marcus. "Still, I think he may not have *intended* to be saucy—that is a fault he is not much addicted to. What did you do with Mrs. Benham's stick, Ronald?"

"I broke it, and threw it into the swamp," replied Ronald.

Marcus expressed a wish to see the blotted writing-book, and it was handed to him. After a close examination, he discovered that the blots were of a lighter color than the writing upon the page, indicating one of two things: 1st, They were made with a different ink from that which Ronald used; or, 2d, They had been recently made, and the ink had not yet acquired its perfect color from contact with the air. This discovery, however, gave no clew to the mystery, although it proved that Ronald did not blot the book when he last used it. Ronald now renewed his protestations of innocence, with such apparent sincerity, that Marcus felt satisfied he was telling the truth, especially as he had not known him to adhere stubbornly to a falsehood for several years. His teacher also admitted the possibility of his innocence so far as that offence was concerned, but thought he had done enough, independent of that, to justify her in excluding him from the school.

"We admit that he has done wrong," said Marcus, "but we should be very sorry to have him expelled from school. He expects to leave next month, but he mustn't go with such a stain as this upon his name. On what conditions will you consent to his coming back to school?"

Mrs. Benham thought a moment, and then replied:—

"I do not wish to be harsh or unreasonable with Ronald. If he is sorry for what he has done, and is willing to say so before the school, that is enough. As the offence was committed before the whole school, I do not think I ought to ask less than that."

"I think that is reasonable," replied Marcus. "Are you willing to do it, Ronald?"

Ronald made no reply until the question had been repeated several times, and then he merely shook his head negatively.

"Well, perhaps he will change his mind before to-morrow morning," said Marcus, addressing the teacher; and bidding her good evening, he started for home, followed by Ronald.

Marcus said little to the boy, on their way home, preferring to leave him to his own thoughts—not very pleasant company to be sure, but perhaps the best for him, under the circumstances. Before Ronald went to bed, however, Mrs. Page talked with him a little while about the affair. There were three classes of motives by which she endeavored to persuade him to comply with the teacher's requirement. First she appealed to his affection for her—a motive that seldom failed to take effect upon Ronald. Then she appealed to reason, and tried to overcome him by argument. Finally she resorted to a lower and more selfish class of motives, and portrayed the disgrace of being expelled from school, and the instantaneous relief of mind he would find in confessing his fault. Still the proud spirit was unsubdued.

After a troubled night, Ronald awoke in quite as unhappy a frame of mind as ever. He went about his morning's work, silently, and the other children, not wishing to intermeddle in his trouble, kept so much aloof that he fancied they shunned him. Oscar, however, remembering a lesson that had recently been impressed upon his mind, cast his influence upon the right side, and advised Ronald to yield. Still the stubborn will revolted at the thought.

It was a settled principle with Mrs. Page, that when a child refuses to be governed by such motives as may be drawn from love, reason, the hope of reward, and the fear of punishment, it is time for authority to assume its stern sway. Having exhausted these motives upon Ronald, in vain, there remained but one other—YOU MUST; and this she proceeded to apply.

"Ronald," she said, a little while before school time, "it is time to be fixing for school; and here is a note which I wish you to take to the teacher."

"Have I got to go to school to-day?" inquired Ronald, in a tone of surprise, as though such a possibility had not occurred to him.

"Yes," replied Mrs. Page, in a calm but firm manner, "you are going to school this morning, and as soon as it opens you will make a public apology for your conduct yesterday. I have written to your teacher that you will do so. You must carry a stick, too, in place of the one you threw away. Marcus will give it to you."

"But what must I say?" inquired Ronald, his eyes swimming with tears.

"Tell her you are sorry for what you did yesterday, and ask her to forgive you. That is all you need say."

With a sad countenance and a heavy heart, Ronald turned his steps towards the school-house. Reluctant though he was to go, he hurried on his way, hoping to reach the school-room before many of the scholars had assembled. He began to realize his unpleasant situation as he noticed that a group of little girls were eyeing him curiously, and evidently making him the subject of remark. Soon a squad of boys noticed his approach, and commenced a volley of rough salutations.

"Halloo, Ron! going to take the rest of that licking to-day?" cried one.

"Ha, old fellow! you'll catch it—I bet you will," said another.

"You've got to be turned out of school—teacher said so," cried out another.

Ronald passed on without replying to his young tormentors, and entering the school-room, deposited the letter and the new ratan upon the teacher's desk. He then took his seat, and tremblingly awaited the opening of the school. Mrs. Benham soon came in, and, after hastily reading the letter, gave the signal for the school to assemble. As soon as the opening exercises were over, Ronald arose, and in a low, tremulous voice said:—

"Mrs. Benham, I am very sorry for what I did yesterday, and I beg your pardon."

Perfect stillness reigned throughout the room, broken only by the sobs of Ronald, as he sat down and burst into tears. The painful silence was quickly relieved by the teacher, who, grasping Ronald kindly by the hand, said, with much feeling:—

"I forgive you, with all my heart, Ronald, and I am glad you have manliness enough to confess your fault, and ask forgiveness. You have acted very honorably, in doing this, and I shall think all the better of you for it, hereafter. We will bury the past and be good friends again," and she gave his hand a new shake. Then turning to the school she continued, "I have a confession to make, too. I am now satisfied that Ronald was not guilty of the offence for which I undertook to punish him yesterday. He says he does not know how his writing-book was blotted, and I believe him. I was too hasty, in punishing him, and am sorry for it. I ask his forgiveness. And I hope the one that blotted the book will come forward and own it, and relieve him from all suspicion of falsehood."

The teacher paused, and looked around the room, but no one responded to the call. She then continued:—

"I am very sorry to think there is one here who can be so dishonorable, and unjust, and mean, as to try to conceal his fault under these circumstances. I am sure he cannot have a very quiet conscience."

The kind, forgiving spirit of the teacher, and her readiness to acknowledge her own error, completely subdued the proud heart of Ronald. He felt truly glad that he had confessed his fault. Indeed, with his present feelings, he would have cheerfully done it, of his own free will. Not only was a heavy burden removed from his mind, but he felt a new and stronger affection for his teacher, realizing the truth of the saying, that "whoever is forgiven much, will love much."

CHAPTER VI.

LETTER-WRITING.

SEVERAL weeks had elapsed, since Oscar's regular daily tasks were set, and he continued to discharge his duties in a satisfactory manner. The wood-pile grew a little, weekly, under his management, and the kitchen was always kept well supplied with fuel. He had become quite expert in cutting hay and feeding the cows and horses, and the latter he cleaned, harnessed and drove, with the air of a veteran horseman. The hogs, of whom he had the principal care, seemed quite contented under their new master, and rewarded his attentions with many grunts of satisfaction, if not gratitude. He had assisted cheerfully in gathering the late crops of the farm, and had even acknowledged that milking the cows was not so disagreeable work as he had imagined. His lessons, also, were for the most part well learned. To be sure they were not very hard, being mostly reviews of studies he had previously gone over. But his natural abilities as a scholar were good, and he learned easily, when he set about it in earnest. The only exercise that gave him serious trouble was the dreaded Saturday's "composition," which, indeed, was more terrible in anticipation than in reality.

"Isn't it almost time to answer some of your letters, Oscar?" inquired Marcus one morning, as the former was about sitting down to his lessons.

"I suppose it is," replied Oscar.

"Let me see," continued Marcus, "you have had letters from your mother, and from Alice, and from Clinton—these have all got to be answered. And then you promised to write to Willie, or 'Whistler,' as you call him, did you not?"

"Yes," replied Oscar.

"I'm afraid you are a rather negligent correspondent," added Marcus. "I wouldn't get into that habit, if I were you. While you are away from home, you will want to hear from your friends occasionally; but if you neglect them, they will be apt to neglect you."

"But I hate to write letters," replied Oscar.

"Do you consider that a sufficient reason for neglecting to answer the letters of your friends?" inquired Marcus.

"No," replied Oscar.

"Neither do I," continued Marcus. "So I think you had better sit right down and attend to your correspondence, to-day, instead of getting any lessons.

You will have time enough to write all four of the letters. You had better go to your chamber, where you will be out of the way of interruption. You have paper and ink, I believe?"

"Yes," responded Oscar.

"That reminds me of something else, that I want to say to you," added Marcus. "I have noticed within a few days that you are getting in the habit of saying 'yes,' 'no,' 'what?' etc., when speaking to your elders. I noticed it yesterday, when you were talking with Mr. Burr, and I have heard you speak to mother and Aunt Fanny in the same way. It is a little thing, I know, but it always sounds unpleasantly to my ears. It is disrespectful, and shows ill breeding. Somehow, I am very apt to form a bad opinion of a boy or girl who speaks in that way. It is my opinion that many a boy has missed a good situation, by just saying 'yes,' 'no,' or 'what?' when he applied for a place, instead of 'yes, sir,' 'no, sir,' or 'what, sir?' That is worth thinking of, if there were no other motive; don't you see it is?"

"Yes—sir," replied Oscar, nearly forgetting the very word they were talking about.

"So far as I am concerned, personally," continued Marcus, "I have no claim to be *sirred* by you, as there is a difference of only a few years in our ages. Still, as your example will have much influence over Ronald, I thought I had better mention the subject to you. Besides, I may become your teacher in a few weeks, and you know 'Master Page' will have to stand upon his dignity a little, in the schoolroom, whether 'Cousin Marcus' chooses to or not. At any rate, I hope you will try to speak respectfully to older people, if you do not to me. There, I wont detain you any longer—you can go to work on your letters as soon as you please."

Oscar went to his room, and, having arranged his paper, ink and pen, sat down by the open window, for it was a mild Indian-summer day. He first read over the letters he was to answer, and then began to think what he should write in reply. But, failing to keep his mind upon the subject before him, his thoughts gradually wandered off, until he quite forgot the business in hand. As he sat in a dreamy mood, gazing upon the hills, prominent among which was Prescott's Peak, with its signal still erect, he descried a large bird sailing majestically through the air, nearly overhead. It was at a great height, but as it approached the hills it descended, and disappeared in the woods near their base. A few minutes afterward it again soared aloft, and, wheeling around the Peak, as if taking an observation of the monument which the boys had erected, it appeared to descend near the summit, where Oscar finally lost sight of it.

Oscar was satisfied that the strange bird was an eagle, and as he sat patiently watching for its reappearance, he thought what a fine shot it offered, and imagined himself on the mountain, gun in hand, stealthily pursuing the noble game. Now it alights upon a tall tree, within rifle-shot. Cautiously the boy-hunter takes aim; "crack!" goes the fowling-piece; and down tumbles the monarch of the air, crashing through the branches of the tree. His feathers are stained with blood; but his fierce eye flashes defiance at his murderer, as he approaches, and with his powerful wing he well-nigh breaks the arm that is stretched out to secure him. After a desperate struggle, he is despatched by a blow from the butt of the weapon, and is borne home in triumph—a heavy task—to the wonder and admiration of the whole neighborhood.

But Oscar's kindling imagination is not satisfied with this feat. It must try again. The bird eludes his gun, but he follows it, and discovers its haunt, on a steep and rocky precipice, near one of the mountain summits. Throwing aside his gun, and grasping such scanty and stunted trees as are at hand, he boldly lowers himself down the frightful chasm. One misstep, the giving way of a single slender twig, would plunge him headlong to destruction; but what cares he for that? There is a prize below, and he is determined to have it. Now he catches a glimpse of the nest, on a narrow, shelving rock, and for the first time discovers that there are two old birds, which, with outspread wings, are guarding their young brood. Undaunted, he descends the steep and slippery rocks, till he is almost within reach of the nest. Now the eagles, roused to fury, fly at him, and with wing, beak and talon commence the assault. Supporting himself by one hand, he uses the other and one foot to ward off the assailants. Long the battle rages, and again and again the adventurous hunter seems almost overcome; but when about to sink down, faint and gasping, the birds, battered and exhausted, give up the contest in despair. The boy seizes the prize, scrambles up the fearful precipice, and hurries home, to raise a brood of eagles.

"But this isn't writing my letters," exclaimed Oscar to himself, suddenly awaking from his day dream. "A whole hour gone, and not a line written yet. Well, I'll go about it, now. I think I'll write to mother first. Let me think— what day of the month is it? I am sure I can't tell—I must run down stairs and find out."

Oscar went down to the sitting-room, and, by referring to a newspaper, ascertained the date. But, before he laid the paper aside, his eye was attracted by the heading of a story, and, on reading a few lines, he became so much interested in it, that he took the journal up to his room, and thought of nothing else until he had finished reading the piece. Then, remembering his neglected task, he hurriedly arranged his paper, and wrote the date and complimentary address. But the ink did not flow freely from his pen, and, taking a sheet of waste paper, he commenced scribbling upon it, to see if he could remedy the trouble. How long he continued this diversion, he was scarcely aware, but at length it was interrupted by a step on the stairs, and a knock at his door. Quickly concealing the well scribbled evidence of his idleness, he bade the visitor walk in, and Marcus entered.

"Well, how do you get along?" inquired Marcus.

"Not very well," replied Oscar. "I have been hindered by one thing and another, ever since I began. To begin with, just after I came up here, I saw an eagle flying over. Didn't you see it?"

"No—but are you sure it was an eagle?" inquired Marcus.

"Why, yes, it must have been an eagle," replied Oscar. "It was the largest bird I ever saw, and I should think he was all of a mile high when he flew over. He lit on the Peak, and that was the last I saw of him."

"Yes, I remember, now,—I did see a hawk over in that neighborhood, and that must have been your eagle," quietly observed Marcus.

Oscar did not relish such a summary disposal of his eagle story, and was about to protest against it, when Marcus inquired how many letters he had finished.

"None," replied Oscar.

"Not one!" exclaimed Marcus; "and is that the beginning of the first letter?" glancing at the sheet which contained the date and address.

"Yes, sir," said Oscar.

"Ah, you have been reading the newspaper, as well as watching hawks," continued Marcus, as his eye fell upon the printed sheet.

"I got that to see about the date," replied Oscar, forgetting that sometimes there is little difference between half of a truth and a lie.

"What *have* you been doing all the forenoon, then?" inquired Marcus.

"The ink is so thick that I couldn't write," added Oscar.

"Let me try it," said Marcus; and he seated himself in Oscar's chair, and, looking for some waste paper, drew out the sheet which his cousin had covered with all sorts of flourishes, figures, puzzles, etc. "I think the ink must flow pretty freely, if it is thick," he quietly added.

Having satisfied himself that the ink was not to blame, Marcus said he was sorry the letters were not finished, as he was expecting to drive over to an adjoining town, in the afternoon, and intended to let Oscar accompany him, if his task was completed. Oscar said he thought he could finish the letters after he got back; but his cousin was far from agreeing with him in this opinion.

"No," said Marcus, "you will hardly get through this afternoon, supposing you work diligently. I think you had better not stop even for dinner, but I will bring you up something to eat, so that you need lose no time. I want you to finish the four letters before you leave the room, if possible."

Oscar hardly knew whether to consider himself a prisoner, or not, so pleasantly had Marcus addressed him. He concluded, however, that it was time to go to work, and was soon deeply engaged in the letter to his mother. Now that his mind was aroused, and his attention fixed, he found no difficulty in writing, and the letter was about completed, when Marcus appeared, with a light repast, instead of the accustomed substantial noonday meal.

"I never feel like writing, after a hearty meal,—so I have brought you a light dinner," said Marcus, setting the tray upon the table.

"What time shall you start?" inquired Oscar.

"In about an hour," was the reply.

"I have got one letter about done," said Oscar, "and I can finish another before you go. Don't you suppose I could finish the other two after we get back?"

"I am afraid not," replied Marcus. "You will have but little time, then, and besides, you wont feel like writing. I think you had better finish your letters before you do anything else. Perhaps you can get them done in season to mail them to-day."

Marcus now withdrew, and in the course of an hour drove off upon his errand. When he returned, he found the family at tea, and Oscar with them.

"Well, Oscar, have you written all your letters?" inquired Marcus.

"Yes, sir, and carried them to the post office, too," replied Oscar.

"Ah, you have been pretty smart—that is, if you didn't make them too short," observed Marcus.

"They are about as long as my letters generally are," replied Oscar

"You found no great difficulty in writing, when you bent your mind down to it, did you?" inquired Marcus.

"No, sir, not much."

"I supposed you wouldn't," continued Marcus. "Mother, I've been thinking of a plan, this afternoon, for making letter-writing pleasant, and I want your opinion of it."

"I think highly of letter-writing as an exercise," said Mrs. Page, "and if you can devise a way to make the children like it, I shall be very glad."

"I can't see what makes boys hate to write letters so—for my part I like to do it," said Kate.

"Yes, I should think you liked it—you write half a dozen billets every day, in school," interposed Otis.

"Why, Otis Sedgwick, what a story! I don't believe I have averaged more than one note a day, this whole term," replied Kate.

"Well, that speaks pretty well for your epistolary taste, if you have done nothing more," said Marcus. "But let me explain my plan. I propose that we have a letter-box put up in some part of the house, and that every one in the family engage to write one letter a week to some other member, and drop it into the box, which we might call our post office. The greatest liberty might be allowed, in the choice of subjects and style, and the letters might be anonymous, or written in an assumed character, if preferred. If any one wanted to ask a favor, or make a complaint, or offer a suggestion, or correct an error, or drop a word of caution or reproof, or indulge a fancy, or make sport, this would afford a good opportunity to do it. What do you think of the plan, mother?"

"I think it is a good idea, and I shall vote for giving it a fair trial," said Mrs. Page.

"And how does it strike you, Aunt Fanny?" continued Marcus.

"Very favorably," replied Miss Lee. "If you can interest the young folks in it, I have no doubt it will work well."

"O, I think it is a capital idea—I shall vote for it with both hands," exclaimed Kate.

"And what say you, Oscar?" inquired Marcus.

"I suppose I must come into the arrangement, if all the others do," replied Oscar, smiling.

"Not much enthusiasm there," observed Marcus; "but we'll excuse him, as he has been writing letters all day. Well, Otis, what do you say to the plan?"

"I hate to write letters," replied Otis.

"Very likely," said Marcus; "and that is precisely the reason why you ought to come into our arrangement, for we are going to try to make letter-writing easy and pleasant."

"Well, I'll agree to it," said Otis.

"Of course you wont hang back, Ronald?" added Marcus.

"I don't know about that," replied Ronald. "Couldn't I be mail-boy, or post-master, or something of that sort, and so be excused from writing?"

"We probably shall not need your services in that line—we can help ourselves to our letters," replied Marcus.

"Well, I'll join your society on one condition," said Ronald, with an air of grave importance.

"What is that?" inquired Marcus.

"That you shan't make us write long letters," was the reply.

"Your letters may be as long or as short as you choose to make them," replied Marcus. "We have all agreed to the plan—now I think it would be well to have a few written rules, to govern us. Perhaps we can arrange that after we get through our work this evening."

The proposal was approved, and in the evening the subject was again brought up. All were invited to offer such suggestions as occurred to them.

"Would it not be well enough for us to resolve ourselves into a society, and adopt a name?" inquired Aunt Fanny.

"I think it would,—what shall we call it?" inquired Marcus.

"The Post Office Society," suggested Otis.

"The Literary Fraternity," proposed Kate.

"The Letter-writing Society," said Mrs. Page.

The latter name was finally adopted, as being more expressive than the others. Aunt Fanny then suggested that the title needed the addition of some qualifying word, to make it more definite and distinctive.

"Call it the Highburg Letter-writing Society," said Kate.

"There are only seven of us, and I doubt whether it would be exactly modest to appropriate the name of the town to our association," remarked Mrs. Page.

"The Page Letter-writing Society," suggested Ronald.

"The Excelsior Letter-writing Society," proposed Kate.

"That is better," said Marcus. "Does anybody object to it? No; so we will call that point settled. Now please to suggest rules for our government."

"Every member must write at least one letter weekly to some other member," said Mrs. Page.

"And if any one fails to contribute his share to the stock of letters, what shall be done to him?" inquired Miss Lee.

"Turn him out," said Otis.

"Debar him from taking any letters from the office, until he has made good all deficiencies," suggested Mrs. Page.

This latter proposal was adopted, and further suggestions called for.

"All letters must be sealed," suggested Kate.

"And pre-paid," added Ronald.

"I hardly think it necessary to seal the letters," said Marcus. "Perhaps we had better leave that optional with the writer."

"But I think the one that receives the letter ought to have something to say about that, as well as the writer," said Kate.

"Well, I have no objection to your rule, if no one else has," said Marcus.

Several other rules were agreed to, and noted down by Marcus. When completed, the list of regulations stood as follows:

"REGULATIONS OF THE EXCELSIOR LETTER-WRITING SOCIETY.

"Each member shall write at least one letter per week to some other member.

"Any member who fails to comply with this rule, without a reasonable excuse, shall forfeit his right to take letters from the post office until his delinquency is made good.

"Each member shall divide his epistolary favors as equally among the others as possible.

"The utmost freedom as to matter and style will be allowed, but nothing must be written calculated to wound the feelings of another.

"Fictitious signatures, and a disguised hand, are allowable, when preferred.

"All letters to be sealed.

"The post office to be accessible to any member, at all times."

CHAPTER VII.

THE RAIN POWER.

AFTER the children had gone to school, the next day, Marcus made a letter-box, and fastened it against the wall, in the entry. While he was at work upon it, a young lady from another part of the town called in to invite the family to a husking party. On learning the design of the box, she solicited the privilege of inaugurating it, which was readily granted. So, begging a sheet or two of paper, she sat down and wrote notes of invitation to Kate, Otis and Ronald, and dropped them into the box.

"Hurrah! here's the post office box, and some letters in it!" exclaimed Ronald, when he came home from school in the afternoon.

"I'm going to have the first one, let me see if I'm not," cried Kate, rushing for the post office.

"No, the first one is for me, but here's one you may have," replied Ronald, handing Kate the note directed to her.

"Well, there's one rule broken, the very first thing—it isn't sealed," said Kate; "and it is written with a lead pencil, too—I don't think that's fair."

She opened the billet, and read:—

> "Miss Jenny Marsh requests the pleasure of Miss Katharine Sedgwick's company at a husking party on Friday evening.
>
> "Oct. 16th."

The notes addressed to Ronald and Otis were in the same form as Kate's. The invitation was quite gratifying to all of the children, and the proposed party occupied a large share of their thoughts and tongues, for the rest of the day. Their ardor was somewhat dampened, however, by Mrs. Page, who told them she thought a storm was near, which might interfere with their arrangements.

"I don't see any signs of a storm—I think it looks real pleasant," said Kate.

"The water boiled away from the potatoes very fast, this noon, and that is a pretty good sign of rain," replied Mrs. Page.

"I don't see what that has to do with rain," said Ronald.

"I can't explain it very clearly," replied Mrs. Page, "but I know it is so. I suppose there is something peculiar in the state of the atmosphere, just before a storm, which makes boiling water evaporate, or fly off into steam, more rapidly than at other times."

The sun rose clear, the next morning, and the children laughed at Mrs. Page for her prediction of rain. But in an hour or two, clouds began to gather, and early in the afternoon a heavy rain commenced. The children came home from school, wet, disappointed, and cross. Every thing seemed to go wrong with them, the rest of the day. Kate had wet her feet, and a grumbling tooth-ache admonished her that she had taken cold. Otis had left his new kite out doors, and found the paper upon it reduced to a handful of pulp, when he came home. The cows chose the luckless day to take a stroll into the neighbors' enclosures, and led Ronald on a long and provoking tramp through the wet grass and soft, spongy lowlands, in search of them. Nor did Oscar escape his share of the ill-luck which seemed to brood over the household; for while milking, one of the cows, nettled perhaps by her long walk and the unpleasant state of the weather, gave him a slap across his eyes with her wet tail that almost took away his sight for a few minutes, at the same time leaving upon his face an embrocation that was not exactly calculated to soothe his ruffled feelings.

"What is the matter? have you all got the blues?" inquired Marcus, at the tea-table, as he observed how gloomy and silent the younger portion of the family appeared.

"O dear, I should think this horrid weather was enough to give any one the blues," exclaimed Kate.

"It doesn't affect me very unpleasantly," replied Marcus.

"Well, you don't care anything about the husking party, I suppose," said Kate.

"Oh, it's the disappointment, and not the weather, that troubles you," observed Marcus.

"Not altogether that, but I think it's too bad we can't go to-night," replied Kate.

"It *is* too bad that all the affairs of this world can't be ordered to suit your convenience," added Marcus.

"No, I don't wish that; but when I make up my mind to go any where, I do want to go," said Kate.

"Which is pretty much the same thing as wishing that Providence would lay all his plans with special reference to your private interests, without regard to the rest of the world."

Kate made no reply, but Ronald came to her rescue.

"I don't believe anybody wants it to rain, now," he said; "the crops are all in, and what good will it do?"

"I think the owners of mills on the rivers could give you a good reason why it ought to rain now," replied Marcus; "and perhaps we should find another reason at the bottom of our wells, after we have used up all the water, a few months hence."

"Well, then, I don't think it need rain so much at a time," said Ronald. "Just hear how it's pouring down now, and it has been raining so almost all the afternoon."

"How much water do you suppose has fallen?" inquired Marcus.

"About a foot, I guess," replied Ronald.

"A foot of rain!" exclaimed Marcus, with astonishment.

"Well, half a foot, certainly," said Ronald.

"No; halve it again, and you will come nearer to the truth," added Marcus.

"What, only three inches? it's more than that, I know," said Ronald.

"I doubt whether you have any idea how much three inches of rain is," replied Marcus. "After tea we will go into a little calculation about it."

When the tea table was cleared away, Marcus proposed that all the children should provide themselves with paper or slates, and see if they could ascertain how much water had fallen in Highburg that day.

"We will assume," he said, "that three inches of rain has fallen, on a level, which I think may be very near the true quantity. The town contains about thirty square miles. Now, the first question is, how many hogsheads of water have fallen on this surface, to-day?"

For a few moments nothing was heard but the clicking and scratching of pencils, and the rustling of the leaves of the arithmetic, by those who were not quite sure they knew the "tables." Those who finished the work first were requested to keep silent till the others had got through. When all were ready, the answers were read off. The solutions of Marcus, Oscar and Kate agreed, and were assumed to be correct; while those of Ronald and Otis were different, and were voted incorrect. Marcus then proposed several other questions in regard to the rain, which led to a series of calculations. The children soon became quite interested in the problems, and were not a little surprised at the facts brought out. Marcus noted down the several answers, on a clean sheet of paper, and the following is a copy of the record:—

"WHAT THE CLOUDS DID IN HALF A DAY.

"The water that has fallen this afternoon and evening, in this town alone, would fill 24,826,775 hogsheads.

"It would measure 209,088,000 cubic feet.

"Its weight is 5,833,928 tons.

"Were this water all in a pond, thirty feet deep, it would be sufficient to float 3,484 vessels, allowing 2,000 square feet to each, or about one-sixth of all the steam and sailing vessels of every class in the United States.

"It would take a man 13,792 years to distribute this water, with a watering pot, supposing he distributed 6 hogsheads a day, and worked 300 days in a year.

"To distribute it in the same time as the clouds, half a day, would require 8,275,590 men, or more than twice as many as voted at the Presidential election of 1856, in the United States.

"It would take $6,206,692 to pay these men for their services, at the rate of $1.50 per day.

"If this water had all fallen to the earth in one solid mass, from a height of one mile, it would have struck the ground with a force of 3,389,512,500 tons."

"There," said Marcus, after reading aloud the foregoing record, "who would have imagined that the clouds were carrying on such an extensive business as that? Isn't it wonderful? And then just think that this storm has extended over perhaps half of the United States. What a deluge of water must have fallen! And this, you must remember, is an account of only one storm—only three inches of rain, out of thirty or forty that we have every year."

"Why! do we have as much rain as that in a year?" inquired Kate.

"Yes," replied Marcus, "our average in this part of Vermont is, I believe, about thirty-two inches, including snow reduced to water. Along the sea coast they have more—in Boston, for instance, about forty inches. There are some parts of the world where they have almost as many feet of rain as we have inches, and nearly all of it falls in about two months of the year, too."[4]

4. According to Prof. Guyot, rain falls at Paramaribo, in Dutch Guiana, to the amount of 229 inches, or 19 feet, annually. There is a place in Brazil where 276 inches, or 23 feet, have fallen in a year. But the greatest quantity ever observed is at an elevated point in British India, south of Bombay, where the enormous amount of 302 inches, or over 25 feet, has fallen in a year. At Cayenne, 21 inches of rain have been known to fall in a single day, or nearly as much as falls in a whole year in the northern latitudes. The annual average fall in tropical America, is 115 inches; in temperate America, 39 inches. The average for the entire surface of the globe is about five feet. These figures may

afford the young arithmetician a basis for a variety of curious calculations, some rainy day, when he is at a loss for amusement, and is disposed to look a little more curiously into the wonderful results of "the rain power."

"What do people do there? I should think they would be all washed away," said Kate.

"No," said Marcus, "it isn't so bad as it seems. It is soon over with, and they have more pleasant days in the year than we do. I suppose they pity us because we have so many stormy days, and yet get so little rain after all. Besides, they know about when their rainy days are coming, and can be prepared for them."

"But, after all," said Aunt Fanny, "I think our arrangement of the weather is best, if it does sometimes interfere with our plans. We generally have all the rain we want, and it is given to us a little at a time, as we need it. This is better for us and for vegetation than to have all our rain fall in two months of the year, and then to have three or four times as much as we really need."

"Then why doesn't God make it rain so every where, if that way is best?" inquired Ronald.

"For wise and good reasons, no doubt," replied Aunt Fanny. "What is best for the temperate zones may not be best for the tropics. People who go from this latitude to tropical countries find the rainy season very unhealthy, but it is different with those who were born there."

"I suppose one object of these heavy rains between the tropics is to supply the great rivers of South America and Africa," said Marcus. "We all know how Egypt is fertilized by the overflowing of the Nile; but the Nile would not overflow were it not for these immense rains in the country where it rises. So with the great rivers of South America, which overflow in the rainy season, and form inland seas, that serve as reservoirs in the dry months."

"And it is so with all the rivers in the world—they are nothing but drains to carry away the surplus rain-water," said Mrs. Page.

"Well," said Marcus, glancing at the figures before him, "we have ascertained that nearly six million tons of water have fallen in our town to-day. Otis, can you explain how this immense body of water was raised into the air?"

"I can explain it," said Kate, seeing that her brother hesitated.

"Let Otis try first," replied Marcus.

"Was it drawn up from the ocean by the sun?" inquired Otis.

"Yes, that is the correct explanation," continued Marcus. "Now, Kate, can you tell us any more about it?"

"The heat of the sun," said Kate, "causes a vapor to go up into the air from the ocean, and lakes, and rivers, and from everything that contains water. This is called evaporation. You can't see this vapor, as it flies away into the air, but when the atmosphere grows cold, it forms clouds, and falls in rain."

"I should think the vapor would all dry up, and be lost, when the air is so warm," said Ronald.

"What do you mean by drying up?" inquired Marcus.

"Why, you know,—I mean drying up,—I can't think of any other way to explain it," replied Ronald.

"When the water in a puddle dries up," said Marcus, "it flies into the air, in the form of a vapor, and that is evaporation. That is all the drying up there is about it. The air steals the water from the puddle, and then keeps it a close prisoner till the cold releases it. The water doesn't dry up again in the air, but remains there. The warmer the air, the more water it will hold. In the tropics, where they have such fierce heats, the air is always full of moisture, and the plants draw it out by means of their large leaves, and so they manage to flourish the year round, although they have no rain or even clouds for months in succession. It is so with us, on a very sultry day,—there is more water than usual in the air, at such a time, although we cannot see it. Now, Kate, can you explain why this vapor which heat produces, flies away to the region of the clouds?"

"Because it is lighter than the air," replied Kate.

"Right," said Marcus.

"You said you couldn't see this moisture rise from the earth," said Aunt Fanny, "but that is not always the case. We see it in our breath, on a cold day, when it looks like steam issuing from our mouths. I have seen a river steaming as though there were a fire under it, in a very cold day, before ice had formed over it. We see this process going on, too, in the vapors or fogs which often collect over ponds, and rivers, and the ocean. But commonly, as Kate says, we see nothing of these vapors until they are condensed into clouds by the cold air above, although they are continually flying off from our bodies, and from the ground, and every thing that grows in it. When we hang out our clothes to dry, after washing them, the water in them goes to help make clouds."

"There is one other agent in this business, that has not been mentioned," said Marcus. "The sun draws the water, the atmosphere holds it as in a sponge, and the cold squeezes the sponge and returns the water to the earth.

But the rain is not needed where it is first collected—it must be transported to distant parts of the earth; and how is this done?"

"By the winds," replied Oscar.

"Yes," resumed Marcus, "the winds are the great water-carriers, that distribute the rain over the earth. Here, then, we have the whole list of forces employed in this wonderful rain power, viz.:

"1. The sun, to draw the water by its heat.

"2. The atmosphere, to hold it.

"3. The winds, to transport it over the continents.

"4. The cold, to discharge it from the clouds when it has reached its destination."[5]

> 5. Strictly speaking, these agents may be reduced to two; for the wind is only air in motion, and cold is not a substance, but merely the absence of heat, as darkness is the absence of light.

"How does the cold make the rain fall?" inquired Ronald.

"It contracts the air," replied Marcus, "and the vapor is consequently condensed, or crowded together, so that its particles unite and form drops of rain, which are heavier than the air, and fall to the earth. As I said before, the atmosphere may be compared to a sponge, which holds a certain quantity of water, in minute particles. When the air sponge is contracted, these particles mingle together and run out, and then it rains."

"What a squeezing the sponge must have had to-day!" exclaimed Ronald.

"When the vapor freezes before it falls to the earth," said Kate, "it becomes snow; and when very cold and very hot and moist air come together, they make hail, or ice."

"I know a riddle about that," said Ronald, repeating:—

"My father is the Northern Wind,

My mother's name was Water:

Old Parson Winter married them,

And I'm their hopeful daughter."

"Did you know that snow-flakes are usually crystals of regular and beautiful forms?" inquired Marcus.

Kate and Oscar had read of this, but it was new to the other children. Marcus took down a volume from the library, and showed to them some drawings of these snow crystals, as seen under a microscope, a few of which are here given. There is an endless variety of these crystals, the most beautiful of which are found in the polar regions; but sometimes the flakes present no traces of crystallization.

"My geography says it never rains in the Great Desert of Sahara; what is the reason of that?" inquired Ronald.

"The Sahara," replied Marcus, "is a vast ocean of sand, in the torrid zone. The air which arises from it is so scorching hot, that it burns up, as it were, the clouds of rain that blow towards it from the Mediterranean, as soon as they come within its reach. There are several other deserts in Africa, and in North and South America. Some of these are cut off from their supply of rain by mountains. When the clouds come in contact with a chain of high mountains, they are driven up their sides, into a colder region, and the vapor is pretty thoroughly wrung out of them. By the time the current of wind reaches the other side of the mountains, the clouds have all disappeared, and there is nothing left but a cold, dry air. That explains why it is that there is a desert region on the western coast of South America, on the very borders of the Pacific Ocean. The eastern sides of the Andes rob the clouds of all the rain brought from the Atlantic by the trade wind, and as the dry wind keeps on its course, the vapors of the Pacific are driven back to the ocean, before they can discharge themselves. Thus there is a paradise on one side of the mountains, and a desert on the other."

"Five minutes of nine," said Mrs. Page, warningly.

"Is it so late?" inquired Marcus. "Well, we will have a bit of poetry to wind up with, and I will appoint Kate to read it aloud, as it is a beautiful piece, and I'm afraid none of the rest of us would do it justice."

"O, you flatterer!" exclaimed Kate.

"No, it isn't flattery,—it *is* a capital poem, if I'm any judge," added Marcus, turning over the leaves of a book in search of the piece. "It's by Bryant—ah, here it is. Now, Miss Kate, let us hear what the poet says about rain, so that we may have something pleasant to dream about, when we go to bed."

Kate took the book, and read in an admirable manner the following lines:—

A RAIN DREAM.

BY WILLIAM CULLEN BRYANT.

THESE strifes, these tumults of the noisy world,

Where Fraud, the coward, tracks his prey by stealth,

And Strength, the ruffian, glories in his guilt,

Oppress the heart with sadness. Oh, my friend,

In what serener mood we look upon

The gloomiest aspects of the elements

Among the woods and fields! Let us awhile,

As the slow wind is rolling up the storm,

In fancy leave this maze of dusty streets,

For ever shaken by the importunate jar

Of commerce, and upon the darkening air

Look from the shelter of our rural home.

Who is not awed that listens to the Rain

Sending his voice before him? Mighty Rain!

The upland steeps are shrouded by their mists;

The vales are gloomy with thy shade; the pools

No longer glimmer, and the silvery streams
Darken to veins of lead at thy approach.
Oh, mighty Rain! already thou art here;
And every roof is beaten by thy streams,
And as thou passest, every glassy spring
Grows rough, and every leaf in all the woods
Is struck and quivers. All the hilltops slake
Their thirst from thee; a thousand languishing fields,
A thousand fainting gardens are refreshed;
A thousand idle rivulets start to speed,
And with the graver murmur of the storm
Blend their light voices, as they hurry on.

Thou fill'st the circle of the atmosphere
Alone; there is no living thing abroad,
No bird to wing the air, nor beast to walk
The field; the squirrel in the forest seeks
His hollow tree; the marmot of the field
Has scampered to his den; the butterfly
Hides under her broad leaf; the insect crowds
That made the sunshine populous, lie close
In their mysterious shelters, whence the sun
Will summon them again. The mighty Rain
Holds the vast empire of the sky alone.

I shut my eyes, and see, as in a dream,
The friendly clouds drop down spring violets
And summer columbines, and all the flowers
That tuft the woodland floor, or overarch
The streamlet:—spiky grass for genial June,
Brown harvests for the waiting husbandman,

And for the woods a deluge of fresh leaves.

I see these myriad drops that slake the dust,
Gathered in glorious streams, or rolling blue
In billows on the lake or on the deep,
And bearing navies. I behold them change
To threads of crystal as they sink in earth,
And leave its stains behind, to rise again
In pleasant nooks of verdure, where the child,
Thirsty with play, in both his little hands
Shall take the cool clear water, raising it
To wet his pretty lips. To-morrow noon
How proudly will the water-lily ride
The brimming pool, o'erlooking, like a queen,
Her circle of broad leaves. In lonely wastes,
When next the sunshine makes them beautiful,
Gay troops of butterflies shall light to drink
At the replenished hollows of the rock.

Now slowly falls the dull blank night, and still,
All through the starless hours, the mighty Rain
Smites with perpetual sound the forest leaves,
And beats the matted grass, and still the earth
Drinks the unstinted bounty of the clouds,
Drinks for her cottage wells, her woodland brooks,
Drinks for the springing trout, the toiling bee
And brooding bird, drinks for her tender flowers,
Tall oaks, and all the herbage of her hills.

A melancholy sound is in the air,
A deep sigh in the distance, a shrill wail

Around my dwelling. 'Tis the wind of night;
A lonely wanderer between earth and cloud,
In the black shadow and the chilly mist,
Along the streaming mountain side, and through
The dripping woods, and o'er the plashy fields,
Roaming and sorrowing still, like one who makes
The journey of life alone, and nowhere meets
A welcome or a friend, and still goes on
In darkness. Yet awhile, a little while,
And he shall toss the glittering leaves in play,
And dally with the flowers, and gaily lift
The slender herbs, pressed low by weight of rain,
And drive, in joyous triumph, through the sky,
White clouds, the laggard remnants of the storm.

CHAPTER VIII.

INSUBORDINATION.

IT was a cherished opinion with Marcus, that the best government for a child is that which teaches him to govern himself. He had derived this notion from his mother and aunt, both of whom, in all their intercourse with the young, had endeavored to keep it in mind. Marcus had put this theory in practice, to some extent, in the management of Ronald, and not without success. He anticipated a still greater triumph of this principle, however, with Oscar, whose age, and peculiar circumstances, seemed favorable to the experiment. Accordingly, instead of fixing metes and bounds for Oscar, and hampering him with set rules and commands, Marcus usually made known his wishes in the form of suggestions, advice, etc., taking it for granted that his will, plainly declared, would be regarded as law by his cousin. And so it was, for a few weeks. But gradually a change came over Oscar. He still attended faithfully to his work and studies, but began to manifest some impatience of control in other matters, and to take advantage of the liberty accorded to him. It was evident that he was falling into the notion that, aside from his stated work and his lessons, he could do pretty much as he pleased.

Marcus noticed this change with no little anxiety and regret. He began to fear that he should be obliged to abandon the self-government theory, at least with Oscar. He kept his uneasiness to himself for a time, but as the evil manifestly increased, he at length broke the subject to his mother. It was at the close of a mild October afternoon. Supper was finished, the cows were milked, and as dusk approached, Oscar was seen to go over towards Mr. Hapley's, and soon after re-appeared, with Sam, with whom he walked rapidly towards the village.

"Mother, how do you think Oscar is getting on? Does he do as well as you expected?" inquired Marcus, as he entered the house, after observing his cousin's movements.

"Why, yes, I do not see but that he is doing pretty well," replied Mrs. Page. "He works better than I supposed he would, and he gets his lessons well, too."

"But don't you think he is a little too much inclined to have his own way?" inquired Marcus.

"I have suspected it was so," replied his mother; "but as you have had the principal management of him, you can judge best about that."

"For instance," resumed Marcus, "I gave him to understand, when he first came here, that we didn't want him to have anything to do with Sam Hapley."

"So did I," interrupted Mrs. Page.

"I never actually forbade him to associate with Sam," continued Marcus, "but Oscar knows what he is, and he knows better than to go with him. And yet they are getting quite intimate. They were off together nearly all the afternoon, yesterday, hunting squirrels, as Oscar says; and this evening he has gone off with him again, notwithstanding I have told him two or three times that we all made it a rule not to be away from home after dark, except by special arrangement."

"I told him the same thing, the last evening he was out," added Mrs. Page.

"He has gone contrary to my wishes in several other matters," resumed Marcus. "There's tobacco, for one thing. I am satisfied that he is beginning to use it again; you know he formed the habit in Boston."

"Yes, but I hope he isn't sliding into it again," said Mrs. Page.

"I think he is," replied Marcus; "in fact, I am very certain he is, for I have smelt tobacco in his breath, several times. I have talked to him about the bad effects of tobacco, but didn't let him know that I suspected he used it. Last Saturday I wrote something on the subject, and addressed it to him, and dropped it into our letter-box. I have got a copy of it—here it is."

Marcus took from his pocket a note, and read it aloud. As it may possibly interest some young reader who is trying to cultivate an acquaintance with tobacco, it is here given entire.

"WHY I DON'T LIKE TOBACCO.

"It does a man no good.

"It is a powerful poison.

"It is injurious to the health, and sometimes fatal to the life, especially of the young.

"It weakens and injures the mind.

"It begets an unnatural and burning thirst, which water will not quench, and thus prepares the way for the intoxicating cup.

"It makes a man a slave to its use, so it is almost impossible for him to abandon it, after a few years.

"It is offensive to all who do not use it.

"It is a letter of introduction to bad associates.

"The use of it is a filthy habit.

"It is an expensive habit.

"The only real advantage arising from the use of tobacco that I ever heard of happened to one of a party of sailors who were wrecked upon the Feejee islands. The savages killed and cooked them all, anticipating a delightful feast; but one of the tars tasted so strongly of tobacco, that they couldn't eat him, and so he escaped a burial in their stomachs. As I intend to keep clear of cannibals, I don't think this solitary fact offers me any inducement to steep and pickle myself in tobacco; therefore I intend to remain an

ANTI-PUFFER-AND-CHEWER."

"I'm afraid it didn't do much good," resumed Marcus, somewhat sadly. "I smelt tobacco in his breath again to-day."

"Well," said Mrs. Page, after a pause, "it will never do to let him go on in this way. I think it will be necessary to tell him very plainly and decidedly, that if he will not restrain himself, we must do it for him. One or the other he *must* submit to, or go back to the Reform School, and the sooner he understands this, the better it will be for us all."

The entrance of the other children put a stop to the conversation; but Mrs. Page's last remark confirmed the conclusion to which Marcus had already reluctantly arrived, and left him no longer in doubt as to the proper course to pursue.

The lamps had been lit nearly an hour when Oscar came in, that evening. Nothing was said to him about his absence at the time; but the next day, taking him alone, Marcus talked long and earnestly to him about the course he was pursuing, and told him very decidedly that he could go on in this way no longer. "If we will not put ourselves under restraint," he said, "others must do it for us. It is so in society, in the school, in the family, and everywhere else. The best form of government is self-government, and there is little need of any other, where that is; but if a man wont practise that, then the strong arm of the law must take him in hand, and compel him to do what he could have done much more pleasantly of his own free will."

Oscar attempted no justification of himself, neither did he acknowledge that he had done wrong. He listened in silence to Marcus, with an expression upon his countenance that at once puzzled and disappointed the latter. It were difficult to say whether shame, sadness or sullenness mingled most largely in the feelings mirrored in his face.

There was a marked change in Oscar's demeanor for several days after this event, though not precisely such a change as Marcus desired to see. He was silent, and carried a moody and sullen look upon his face, which did not escape the notice even of the children, although they knew nothing of its cause. Marcus treated him as kindly as ever; but how he longed to look into that troubled heart, and read the thoughts and feelings that were stirring its depths!

About this time a new wonder suddenly appeared in town. The children came home from school with glowing accounts of a mammoth poster or show-bill exhibited outside of the post office, and covering a good portion of one side of the building. It was printed in all kinds of gay colors, and besprinkled from top to bottom with pictures, representing men, women and horses performing all manner of wonderful feats. They also brought home some small bills that had been scattered among the children. It was very seldom that a circus found its way into the small and secluded village of Highburg, but it was pretty evident that one was coming now, "for one day only," and that the children were well-nigh bewitched with the highly-colored descriptions of the entertainment given by the great poster.

There was a decided drawing down of faces, when Mrs. Page informed the excited group that she did not consider the circus a suitable place for them to visit, and could not consent to their going. Some of them were even disposed to question her position.

"Why," said Otis, "mother would let us go, if she were here."

"I do not know about that," replied Mrs. Page; "and therefore I must act according to my own judgment."

"I don't see what harm there could be in our going just once," remarked Kate.

"We ought not to go to an improper place even 'just once,'" replied Mrs. Page. "Circus performers are generally a low class of men and women; their entertainments are low and degrading; and the dregs of the community usually gather around them. Those are the reasons why I do not wish you to go to such a place."

"You've been to the circus, haven't you, Oscar?" inquired Ronald.

"Yes, I have been a good many times," replied Oscar.

"And you agree with me, in your opinion of it, don't you?" inquired Mrs. Page.

"I don't know—I always liked to go pretty well," replied Oscar.

This remark gave Mrs. Page much uneasiness, and she took the first opportunity, when Oscar was alone, to caution him against saying anything in the presence of the children that would excite their desires to go to the circus; a request which he promised to comply with.

The circus paraded through the town on the appointed morning, with its wagon-load of noisy horn-blowers and drum-beaters, and its procession of fancy carriages and fine horses. The great tent was pitched, in the presence of all the idlers of the village, and in due time the door was opened to the public, and the performance commenced.

Oscar finished his work and lessons as early as possible, in the afternoon, and then quietly slipped away from home, without the knowledge of any one. He turned his steps towards the village, where the circus was encamped. He wished merely to see what was going on, and did not intend to venture within the tent, since his aunt was so strongly opposed to such places of amusement. On reaching the circus grounds, he found a motley crowd assembled, composed chiefly of young men and half-grown boys, with a sprinkling of women and young children. There were few representatives of the better class of the population to be seen; but that marvel of laziness, old 'Siah Stebbins, was there, leaning against a fence, with his hands in his pockets; and so was Gavett, the man who once served three months in the county jail for stealing wood; and so were poor Silly John, the pauper, and Tim Hallard, the drunkard, and Dick Adams, the loafer *par excellence*, and little Bob Gooden, swaggering about with a cigar in his mouth, and Sam Hapley, swearing faster than ever, and his brother Henry, eagerly taking lessons in vice. All these were on the field, and others of like character. Some of the boys were mimicking performances they had witnessed inside the tent— turning somersets, standing on their hands, leaping, twisting their bodies into unaccountable shapes, etc.

Two donkeys belonging to the circus, mounted by boys, were driven around the field at a furious pace. A donkey being a novel sight to most of the people, the race attracted much attention from the outsiders, and served admirably to tole them into the enclosure—the object intended.

As Oscar was sauntering about, he came unexpectedly upon Otis, who, with several others of the academy boys, hastened over to the circus, as soon as dismissed, "to see what was going on."

"What, are you here? I thought aunt told you to go right home when school was dismissed," said Oscar.

"I'm going right home," replied Otis, adding, to himself, "I rather think I've just as good a right here as you have."

A moment after, as Otis was still standing by the side of Oscar, there came along a boy about the age of the latter, foppishly dressed, and with a bold face and a careless, swaggering air. His eyes met Oscar's, and there was an instant recognition.

"What, is that you, Alf!" exclaimed Oscar.

"Halloo, Oscar, is that you!" cried the other.

"How came *you* here—do you belong to the circus?" inquired Oscar.

"Yes," replied the other; "but how came *you* here? I thought you were in the house of correction, or some such place. How did you get out of that last scrape, say? O, I remember, they sent you to the Reform School, didn't they?"

Oscar, confused and distressed by this unexpected exposure, made signs to the other to desist, and attempted to turn off the affair as a joke. The strange remark of the strange boy, however, attracted the attention of Otis and several others of Oscar's acquaintances who were standing by, and set them to wondering.

The real name of Oscar's new-found acquaintance was Alfred Walton, but he figured on the circus bills as "Master Paulding." For years the two boys lived near each other, in Boston, and had been very intimate, their tastes and habits being much alike. The hotel and stables kept by Alfred's step-father had been one of Oscar's favorite resorts, and there he learned many of the bad lessons which he was now trying to forget. He had heard nothing from Alfred for a long time, but now learned from him that he quarrelled with his step-father and ran away from home five or six months previous, and being familiar with horses, had since followed the career of a circus rider.

"And look here," added Alfred, taking Oscar aside, "if you want a chance, I'll speak a good word for you to the old man. I shouldn't wonder if he would take you on trial—I bet I can put him up to it. We've got a good company—they are a high old set of fellows, I tell you."

"O no, I can't join you—I've engaged to stay here two or three years," replied Oscar.

"Pooh, never mind that—you can slip off easily enough, just as I did," said Alfred, who seemed to have no idea that any thing but force could hold a person to an engagement with which he was dissatisfied.

"But I don't want to slip off—I like here, well enough," added Oscar.

"Then you must have altered amazingly, if you can content yourself in such a horribly dull hole as this," rejoined Alfred. "Why, I'd hang myself before I'd stay here three weeks. Come, you like to see the world as well as the rest of us do. Say you'll go, and I'll speak to the old man. He'll give you twelve or fifteen dollars a month, as soon as you get broke in a little. That's better than you can do here, I know. What do you get now, any how?"

"I don't have wages—father pays my board, and I'm going to school this winter," replied Oscar.

"Well, I should think you'd rather be your own man, and have a chance to see the world, than be cooped up in the woods here, two or three years," added Alfred. "But come in, or you wont get a seat—performances begin in five minutes," he added, drawing out a watch, to which was attached a flashy chain.

"No, I didn't intend to go in—the folks wont know where I am," replied Oscar.

"Yes, you are going in, too—it wont cost you anything—I'll put you through," said Alfred, pushing Oscar towards the door.

Oscar was unable to withstand the pressing invitation of his old comrade, and suffered himself to be led into the enclosure, where he remained through the entire performance, which did not close until nearly dark. His prolonged absence was noticed at home, and led to unpleasant suspicions; but as Otis remained silent, for fear of exposing himself, nothing definite was known of his whereabouts.

Oscar hurried home with many misgivings, after the exhibition had concluded, and was agreeably surprised to find the supper table still standing for him, and was yet more gratified that no questions were asked in relation to his absence. When he went up to bed, however, Marcus accompanied him to his chamber, and the following conversation took place:—

"Oscar, where have you been this afternoon?"

"Over to the circus."

"Did you go in, or only remain outside?"

"I went in."

"I am very sorry to hear it, and surprised too. You knew it was much against our wishes, did you not?"

Oscar made no reply.

"You knew neither mother nor I would have consented to your going to such a place, did you not?" continued Marcus.

"I supposed you wouldn't."

"Then why did you go? Do you intend to pay any regard to our wishes, or do you mean to have your own way in everything?"

Oscar remained silent.

"Do you remember what I said to you a few days ago, about your behavior?"

"Yes, sir."

"Well, I suppose all it is necessary for me to say now, is, that I intend to abide strictly by what I said at that time. Your going to the circus was to all intents an act of wilful disobedience, and as a punishment, I shall have to declare you a prisoner for the rest of the week."

Oscar did not appear much pleased with this announcement, and something like an expression of anger flitted across his countenance, but he made no reply.

"I do not intend to make you a *close* prisoner," continued Marcus. "I shall let you go on parole, if you agree to that arrangement. I suppose you know what that means."

"It means that I can go at large, if I'll agree not to go off," said Oscar.

"Yes," replied Marcus, "you have the idea. When a prisoner of war is released on parole, he gives his word of honor that he will not go beyond certain fixed limits, and that he will not take part in any hostile act. As we are not at war, we can dispense with the latter part of the bargain. All I shall require is, that you will give me your word of honor not to go beyond certain limits I shall name, without special leave from me, during the rest of this week. You can have your choice between this, and being kept a close prisoner in the house. Which do you choose?"

"To go on parole."

"And do you give your word of honor?"

"Yes, sir."

"Well, you may consider yourself on parole, from this time," added Marcus, and he mentioned the limits beyond which he was not to pass.

"Supposing I should go beyond the limits—what then?" inquired Oscar, who was beginning to regard the deprivation with curiosity rather than displeasure.

"I can suppose no such thing," replied Marcus. "The parole system takes it for granted that when a man deliberately gives his word of honor that he will do a certain thing, he will regard his promise as sacred and inviolable, come what may. If it were not so, there would be an end to the parole, very quick. I believe it seldom happens that a man is found base enough to abuse the parole. I read an account a few days ago, however, in the Life of Napoleon, of some soldiers who broke their parole, but they were Turks. During one of Napoleon's campaigns in Syria, he captured ten or twelve hundred Turkish troops, and released them on parole. Soon after, they were again taken prisoners, while defending a city. A council of war was held, and after considering the matter three days, it was unanimously decided that the prisoners must die. Accordingly they were led out in small groups and shot; and it is said that the pyramid of their bones remains in the desert to this day. But this is a very rare case, and I shall take it for granted that you will keep your promise. In fact, I have so little doubt of it, that I shall not watch you in the least, nor take any pains to find out where you go. If you go outside of the limits, I probably shall not know it, unless I discover it accidentally."

"Well, you may depend on my keeping within the bounds, unless I should forget myself," replied Oscar.

Oscar faithfully kept his parole, through the two remaining days of the week. Under the kind and forbearing yet firm treatment he had received from Marcus, his feelings now began to relent, somewhat, and, despite the mitigating circumstances in the case, which he had not explained to any one, he felt some reproaches of conscience for the course he had pursued. On Saturday afternoon, he half resolved to acknowledge his fault to Marcus, freely and frankly, and ask forgiveness; but when the opportunity came to do so, a false pride overcame the better promptings of his heart, and stifled the words that were trembling on his lips. The quick eye of Marcus, however, perceived that a change had been wrought in the feelings of his pupil, and greatly did he rejoice at it.

CHAPTER IX.

CORRESPONDENCE.

THE "Excelsior Letter-writing Society" had now been in operation several weeks, and had thus far proved a popular and useful institution. The letter-box was regularly patronized by all its members, but one of them having brought upon himself the dire penalty of exclusion from it, and he for only a single day. I do not intend to expose the delinquent, but justice requires me to say it was neither Oscar nor Ronald. The letters which passed through the domestic post office were as various as the writers and their moods. Some were long, and some brief; some serious, and others funny. There were letters advisory, admonitory, commendatory, critical, mysterious, romantic, and quizzical; but none that were disrespectful or unkind, care having been taken to guard against these faults.

A few days after the events narrated in the preceding chapter, Marcus received a letter which afforded him peculiar gratification. It was from Oscar, and was as follows:

"Nov. 6th, 185—.

"DEAR MARCUS,—I think you would not have blamed me so much as you did for going to the circus, last Thursday, if you had known all the circumstances. I did not intend to go inside, when I went over to the village; but I met a boy there named Alfred Walton, that I used to be very intimate with in Boston. He belongs to the company, and tried to persuade me to join them, but I told him I did not wish to. Then he insisted upon my going in, and would not take no for an answer. He got me inside the tent, before I could get away from him. He told the doorkeeper I was his friend, and he let me in without paying. I am very sorry I went near the circus at all; but I could not very well help going in, after I saw Alfred.

"I must tell you about another thing that has troubled me a good deal. Alfred was mean or thoughtless enough to plague me about being sentenced to the Reform School, right before Otis and several other boys that know me. I turned it off as well as I could, but Otis has spoken to me about it since, and I am afraid he thinks there is something in it. I had to tell him what I suppose some people would call 'a white lie,' to get rid of him. I don't see how I can keep the thing from coming out, unless I lie right up and down about it.

"I have thought much lately of what you said about self-government. I like your ideas, and I mean to try to put them in practice. If you could give me any hints that would help me in making the experiment, I should be very thankful.

"Yours truly, OSCAR."

To this letter, Marcus replied as follows, at his earliest convenience:

"HIGHBURG, Nov. 7, 185—.

"DEAR COUSIN OSCAR,—I have not received a more welcome letter for many a day, than yours of yesterday. The extenuating circumstances you mention, in regard to your visit to the circus, change my opinion of that act very much, as you may well suppose; for I thought you went deliberately, and of your own choice. You ought to have explained this before, and I wonder that you did not. Still, I do not think this plea wholly excuses you, unless you were actually *forced* in, which I suppose you do not pretend; and even in that case, you need not have remained in, after Alfred left you. So I must still believe that you were to some extent blameworthy, first, for putting yourself in the way of temptation by going to the circus grounds; and secondly, for yielding to the coaxings of your old friend. I am glad you see your error, and are sorry for it.

"As to keeping certain parts of your history secret, I do not think it a matter of so much importance as you probably do. If you behave well now, and for the future, these errors will soon be forgotten; but if they cannot be concealed without falsehood, I would not attempt to hide them. I would rather acknowledge the facts to Otis, and appeal to his honor and generosity to keep them secret. I think he would not betray you.

"I am rejoiced to learn that you mean to govern yourself. I wish I could help you in this noble work. You must imagine yourself a governor, appointed over a province. Your subjects are the various powers of your mind, the qualities of your heart, your habits, tastes, affections, etc. It is taken for granted that you know something of the law you are to administer. The Bible and your conscience will give you all the instruction you need on this point. The next thing to be done, is to make yourself thoroughly acquainted with the people of your little province. Who are they? What is their character? Are they a hard set to govern, or the contrary? How can you best manage them? This is *self-examination*, and without it, we can neither know ourselves, nor govern ourselves. Well, after we understand pretty well what kind of subjects we have got to deal with, the next thing is to apply the law to them, firmly, vigorously, with unwearied watchfulness, and with a determination to conquer them. We must persevere in this until we accomplish our purpose, and our rule in our own little household is securely established.

"Let me give you a familiar illustration. In looking over the little inner kingdom I am called to rule, we will suppose that I find one subject that has proved quite troublesome. His real name is Laziness, but we will call him by his polite name, Mr. Ease. I can see very plainly, as I examine the past, that I owe to him a great many wasted hours and opportunities, and a great many good things *not* done. Well, one cold winter morning, I astonish Mr. Ease very much by informing him, before my eyes are fairly open, that I intend to rise instanter. This is something very strange, and he begins to expostulate, and to plead for a few moments more in the warm bed; but before he can finish his plea, I am up, and half dressed. 'You are not going to make the fire—your mother can do that,' says Ease, as I go into the kitchen; 'But I *am* going to make it,' I reply, and at it I go, at once. Then I go out to the barn, and see to the stock; but before the morning work is half done, Mr. Ease says, in his blandest voice, 'Come, go into the house, and warm yourself, and get ready for breakfast. This is cold work—let the boys finish it.' I pay no attention to his advice, but keep about my work until it is done, and have all the better appetite for my breakfast, for doing so. After that meal, Mr. Ease kindly reminds me that I have not read the magazine that came yesterday, and suggests that I might spend an hour very comfortably with it in the chimney corner, on such a cold morning. But I tell him it is a clear, bright day, and there is plenty of work to do, and at it I go, without further parley. After dinner, Mr. Ease again intrudes himself, in his blandest way. 'Come,' he says, 'you've worked hard all the forenoon, now put the horse into the sleigh and have a ride; the afternoon is fine, and the sleighing excellent.' 'Ah, yes, the sleighing *is* good,' I reply; 'I think I'll improve it by hauling a load or two of wood, and take the ride some other time.'

"So I keep 'snubbing' this Mr. Ease, as coolly as you please, day after day. Finding he is losing his power over me, he grows shy and glum, and slinks away, and at length I hear but very little from him. He is conquered. And if I find any other upstarts or usurpers in my dominions, I serve them in the same way. If I can't snub them into submission, as I did Mr. Ease, I just seize them firmly by the throat, and choke them down. That is the way I served Mr. Anger.

"To do all this, you must rely upon principle, not impulse. You must form a fixed purpose to govern yourself, and adhere to it, through thick and thin. You must also be willing to submit to some self-denial and sacrifice. Don't be frightened at those words. They look like bugbears, but after all, they are at the root of all our happiness. Almost our first and last experience of life is that of desires denied. From infancy to old age, we are daily and almost hourly called to sacrifice a lesser for a greater good; and until we yield cheerfully to this great law, we have not learned to live, nor have we known true happiness. Self-indulgence and ease make puny, vicious and unhappy men. Self-control and self-denial make strong and noble souls—the master spirits that rule the world.

"I will add but one thought more. However painful the effort at self-government may be, at first, the power of habit will gradually render the work easy, until at length it will actually become a pleasure.

"Wishing you much success in your good purpose, I remain

"Your affectionate cousin,

"MARCUS."

It was not often that so long and formal a letter as this found its way into the family post office. Most of the missives exchanged between the members of the society, were brief notes, a few specimens of which are given:

"MARCUS PAGE, ESQ.—Dear Sir,—I propose that we take the hay-cart, Saturday afternoon, and all hands go off after nuts. What say you to the plan?

"Yours truly, OTIS.
"Oct. 25th."

"O, fie, Ronald! how could you say, 'I intended to have wrote!' It is perfectly barbarous. 'I intended to have written,' is what you should have said. 'I got my lessons' is bad, too; you mean you *learned* your lessons. Please put two t's in regretted, next time, and write Friday with a capital F. But I wont play the critic any more, just now, for fear you might banish from your list of correspondents

"Your faithful friend, KATE.
"Nov. 2."

To this note Kate received the following reply, the next day:

"O, fie, Kate! how could you say, 'I intended to have written!' It is perfectly barbarous. 'I intended to *write*' is what you should have said. If you don't believe me, I can show you the rule in the grammar. Don't be afraid to 'play the critic'—I *like* to have you do it!

"Yours in fun, RON.
"Nov. 3."

Ronald was not accustomed to take things upon trust, especially from one near his own age, when he could conveniently verify their truth for himself. This habit led him to investigate the blunders pointed out by Kate, and the result was, that he was able to convict his critic of a serious grammatical error—a "turning of the tables" which he enjoyed with a roguish zest. Kate did not need to consult the grammar, to satisfy herself in regard to the error; for she at once recalled to mind the rule she had learned: "All verbs expressive of hope, desire, intention, or command, must invariably be followed by the present, and not the perfect of the infinitive."

The post office sometimes served as a medium through which an uneasy conscience sought relief, as in the following:—

"HIGHBURG, Oct. 26th.

"DEAR MISS LEE,—I don't know what you think of me, for speaking to you so rudely, last evening. I was only in fun, of course, but I suppose I carried it too far. I was sorry for it a minute after. I hope you will excuse me, this time, and I will be more careful in future.

"Ever yours,

KATE."

Kate, in a merry mood, had rallied Miss Lee upon her state of singleness, applying to her the epithet, "old maid," and using other expressions that were not quite proper, considering the differences between their ages; hence this apology. Miss Lee, it should be added, was loved and esteemed none the less by those who knew her, because of the peculiarity of which Kate made sport. She was an especial favorite with the children of the family, and her pleasant words and looks, her obliging disposition, her sound advice, her clear explanations of school lesson and other mysteries, her inexhaustible fund of anecdote and story, and not least, the beautiful productions of her pencil and brush, constituted an attraction which all felt and acknowledged. She had spent many years in teaching, but had now relinquished the profession. Her services as an artist were highly appreciated by the children, who coaxed many a pretty drawing or painting from her portfolio. Her letters were eagerly sought for, as they sometimes contained the fruits of her pencil, as well as of her pen. Here is one of them:—

"Nov. 4.

"DEAR OTIS,—Enclosed I send the drawing of the four dogs, which you wished me to make for your little brother. When you forward it to him, you had better call his attention to the dotted lines, otherwise he might not understand the design of the picture. If he should get a piece of tracing paper, he might easily make for himself a separate copy of each of the four dogs. I have not had a letter from you yet. Won't my turn come soon?

"Your friend sincere,

"FANNY."

Here is a copy of the picture enclosed in this letter:

Thus did the domestic post office serve alike to entertain the younger members of the family, and to educate their minds and hearts. Its novelty had not yet begun to wear off, and it was regarded by all as one of the established institutions of the family.

CHAPTER X.

A WOUNDED CONSCIENCE.

MRS. PAGE and Marcus were riding in the outskirts of the town, one afternoon, when they stopped a few moments at the door of an acquaintance—a lady named Blake. She was a widow, and had a large family of children. One of them, a girl named Ellen, was standing near the horse, when her mother remarked—

"I wish I could find a place for Ellen, this winter. If she couldn't earn anything more than her board, it would be better than nothing."

"How old are you, Ellen?" inquired Marcus.

"Thirteen last spring," replied the girl.

"Do you want to go away to live?" asked Mrs. Page.

"I don't know," replied Ellen, with considerable hesitation.

"No, she would rather stay at home," interposed her mother; "but I think she is getting old enough to do something for herself. She could make herself quite useful to any one, if she tried."

"So I should suppose," said Mrs. Page. "Perhaps I can think of some one who would like to take her this winter—I will let you know, if I do."

"Mother," said Marcus, on their way home, "wouldn't it be a good plan for you to take Ellen to help you, this winter? Our family is so large, now, that I think you and Aunt Fanny ought to have some help. Ellen could make the beds, and set the table, and wash the dishes, and do a good deal of other work. Mrs. Lane says she is quite handy about housework. She had the whole management of the family affairs nearly a fortnight, last summer, when her mother was sick."

Mrs. Page did not then make any very definite reply to this proposition, although the same idea had occurred to herself, when Mrs. Blake spoke of Ellen. After thinking and talking the matter over for a few days, and making the necessary inquiries about Ellen, it was decided that she might come to live with them for the winter, if she chose. Marcus accordingly despatched to inform Mrs. Blake of the opening they had made for her daughter. The offer was gratefully accepted, especially as Marcus assured her that Ellen would probably have time and facilities for continuing her studies, the same as if she were attending school. It was agreed that she should be in readiness for her new home, the next week.

The district school which Ronald attended was now near the end of the fall term. It was to close with a public examination and exhibition, for which considerable preparation had been made. Several prizes were to be awarded, for good behavior and scholarship. Among others, a favorite book was to be given to the boy who showed the neatest kept and best executed writing-book at the close of the term. A similar prize was offered to the girls, and another to the scholar whose book showed the greatest improvement, during the term. For the first-named prize Ronald had been a candidate, until the unfortunate blotting of his book, which threw him out of the contest. On the day before the exhibition, as the teacher was making a final examination of the writing-books, she was surprised and vexed to observe several fresh blots upon the book which she supposed would take the prize. It belonged to Lewis Daniels, a boy who sat by the side of Ronald. He denied all knowledge of the matter, however, and could hardly believe that it was his book that was disfigured, until he had seen it for himself. When told that these blots had probably lost him the prize, he did not manifest much emotion; and, indeed, he seemed to take the affair so coolly, from first to last, that Mrs. Benham, the teacher, did not know what to think of it. She at length determined to have some further conversation with him on the subject, and with this purpose detained him after school was dismissed.

"Lewis," she said, when they were alone, "to-morrow is probably the last day that I shall ever be your teacher. I want to part pleasantly with all my scholars, and to carry away agreeable recollections of them. But I feel a little troubled about you. I am afraid you have not told me the truth about your writing-book, and I can't bear to think you are going to bid me good-by with a falsehood in your mouth. Now if you have tried to deceive me, I want you to confess it all, and be forgiven, for I shall not punish you, as we are about to separate."

Lewis colored deeply, and replied in a husky voice—

"I told you all I knew about it."

"But you told me nothing about it," replied Mrs. Benham, whose suspicions were further excited by this reply.

"I know nothing about it," added Lewis.

"Lewis Daniels," continued the teacher, mildly, after a slight pause, "can you look me calmly in the eye, and say that? No, I knew you could not. You cannot act out such a black falsehood. Your manner betrays you. Now will you acknowledge the whole truth?"

"I blotted the book myself," said Lewis, bursting into tears.

"How did it happen?" inquired Mrs. Benham.

"I did it on purpose, because I didn't want to take the prize," sobbed the boy.

"That is a very singular reason—I hope you will not tell me any more untruths about the matter," replied the teacher, mildly, a shade of anxiety flitting across her face.

"It is nothing but the truth, as true as I'm alive," continued Lewis; "I didn't want to get the prize away from Ronald—that's why I did it."

"That was very generous in you, if you are telling the truth," replied the teacher; "but was it just to yourself? If you fairly earned the prize, why should you give it up to another?"

"I didn't earn it fairly," replied Lewis, amid fresh tears and sobs. "I thought he would get the prize, and so I blotted his book one morning, before he got to school. You punished him for it—don't you remember?"

Mrs. Benham did remember, and it would be hard to say whether she or her conscience-stricken pupil suffered most at the recollection of the trying scenes thus recalled, the mystery of which was now unfolded to her. It was not strange that her own tears mingled with those of the sobbing boy, for she felt that she too had erred, though she hoped innocently.

"My poor boy, you have been most severely punished for your fault," at length resumed Mrs. Benham. "Conscience is a stern judge. 'A wounded spirit who can bear?'"

"Yes, ma'am, when you punished Ronald, and when he got up before the school and asked your pardon"—but the penitent boy's emotions were too deep to allow him to finish the sentence.

"And I suppose you have been suffering more or less from this concealed sin, every day since, now about six weeks," said Mrs. Benham.

"Yes, ma'am," replied Lewis. "I felt so mean that I used to keep out of Ronald's way as much as I could. I hated to see him. Then I tried to treat him as well as I could, but that didn't help me much. So I made up my mind at last that I would serve my writing-book the same way that I served his."

"And did you expect to gain peace of mind in this way—by committing another fault, and covering it over with a falsehood?" inquired the teacher. "Your last error was almost as bad as the first. I hope this will be a lesson to you, as long as you live. By delaying this confession so many weeks, you have caused yourself a great deal of suffering, and got further into trouble than you were at first. But as I promised, I cheerfully forgive all, so far as it concerns me. Do you think there is any one else whose forgiveness you ought to seek?"

"I suppose I ought to tell Ronald about it, and ask him to forgive me," replied Lewis.

"I should do so, most certainly," said the teacher; "and you had better see him to-night, if possible, as you may not have an opportunity to speak with him to-morrow. Is there any one else whose forgiveness you propose to seek?"

"I don't know," replied Lewis, in doubt.

"Don't you think your Heavenly Father will expect you to confess this matter to him, and ask his forgiveness?" inquired the teacher. "You have sinned against him quite as much as against Ronald or me. Are you in the habit of praying to him?"

"No, ma'am—only I say a hymn sometimes, when I go to bed," replied Lewis.

"I am sorry you do not pray to him," resumed the teacher. "He made you, and he gives you every good thing you receive, and when you do wrong, he is grieved. I should think you would thank him every day for the blessings he gives, and ask him for those things you need; and when you displease him, I wonder how you can help asking him to forgive you, and to keep you from falling into sin again. Will you join with me, now, in seeking his forgiveness?"

Lewis bowed assent, and knelt down with his teacher, who offered a brief and fervent prayer in his behalf, that his sins might be truly repented of and forgiven, and that he might be kept from transgression hereafter. She then urged him to seek the divine forgiveness, in secret prayer at home, and with a kindly good-night, they separated.

Lewis went directly to Mrs. Page's, where he found Ronald, in company with the other children. After a little while, he managed to draw him aside, saying—

"Come out this way, Ronald—I've got something to tell you."

"Well, tell away," replied Ronald.

"You know the teacher found some blots on my writing-book, this afternoon?"

"Yes—how came they there?"

"I blotted it myself."

"You did? Then you told a whopper."

"I did it purposely, too."

"Then you was a fool. Why, you might have taken the prize, if you hadn't done it."

"But I did something worse than that."

"What was it?"

"I blotted your book the other day, so I might make sure of the prize."

"You mean——" but the hasty reply was instantly checked by a glance at the sorrowful face before him, and Ronald stood silent and ashamed.

"I'm sorry for it, and I hope you will forgive me," added Lewis, the tears gathering in his eyes. "I told the teacher all about it, and she has forgiven me."

"O yes, I'll forgive you, too, seeing you have owned up of your own accord."

"I've suffered enough for it to be forgiven, at any rate."

"You blotted your book so as to be even with me? Well, that was doing the handsome thing, any way. You might have kept dark, and got the prize, just as easy as not. I never supposed any one blotted my book on purpose; I thought it was an accident."

Lewis repeated his expressions of sorrow for his offence, and received renewed assurances of forgiveness. He then returned home with a lighter heart than he had known for many a day.

The examination of the school, the next day, passed off very successfully. A goodly company of visitors was present, the order and general behavior of the scholars were excellent, the classes appeared well, and the singing and declamations were attractive. Ronald, unexpectedly to himself, bore off two of the honors—one for general progress in his studies, and the other for the neatest writing-book. Both prizes were books adapted to his age. As the writing prize was handed to him, the committee-man who distributed the gifts, remarked that his book was somewhat blotted; but as it had been ascertained that it was through no fault of his, and as, saving this fault, his book stood the highest, they had decided to award him the prize. So ended Ronald's last day at the district school. He was now to enter the academy.

CHAPTER XI.

IN-DOOR AMUSEMENTS.

THE fall term of the academy closed a few days after the district school, and Oscar, also, was released from his lessons, so that all the young folks were now having a short vacation. Kate and Otis, however, were greatly disappointed, on receiving a letter from their father, a few days before the term closed, stating that they were to remain in Highburg through the vacation, instead of visiting their home. The serious illness of their little sister was the reason given for this new arrangement, and as a partial offset to the disappointment, their parents promised to make them a brief visit at the earliest possible day.

The weather was now cold, and often dull or stormy, rendering out-door amusements unpleasant, and much of the time impracticable. Marcus, though busily engaged in finishing up his work for the winter, was untiring in his efforts to relieve the disappointment of Kate and Otis, by finding amusements for them and the other children. When the weather would not admit of a ride in the wagon, an excursion in the woods, or a frolic in the fields and on the hill-sides, he was always ready with some game or amusement that could be played in the house or barn. The long evenings, too, were beguiled with innocent and often instructive diversions, and when the wind raved loudest without, there were no gloomy hearts within.

"I'm going to propose a new play," said Marcus, one evening, as the little party gathered around the table; "it is called *Conglomeration.*"

"Conglomeration! I hope the play is as funny as the name," said Kate.

"We shall see," observed Marcus, as he distributed some slips of paper among the children. "Now I want each of you to write five words on separate pieces of paper, and throw them all in a heap on the middle of the table. You can select any words you choose."

When all had written, Marcus mixed together the bits of paper, and then directed each one to take five words from the heap, as they happened to come, and to write one or more sentences containing those words in the order in which they were drawn from the pile.

There was a good deal of merriment among the party, as they glanced at the slips, and perceived what a droll "conglomeration" they had got to weave together. Here are some specimens of them:—

KATE'S.	ROLAND'S.	OSCAR'S.	OTIS'S.

Poetry,	Spider,	Shoot,	Funny,
Physic,	Book,	Gravy,	Toothache,
Should,	Sober,	Girl,	Jewsharp,
Ronald,	Cannot,	Onions,	Going,
Broomstick	Turkey.	Sublime.	Jericho.

No one thought of saying "I can't," however, and in a few minutes, after some rubbing of foreheads and scratching of heads, the last of the sentences was completed.

"Now each one may read his own sentence aloud, emphasizing the words that were given. Otis, we will begin with you."

Otis read:—

> "It would be *funny* if the *toothache* could be cured with a *jewsharp*, but I am not *going* to *Jericho* to find out about it."

"No, I should not," said Marcus; "now, Ronald, what have you written?"

Ronald then read:—

> "The *spider* may not care anything about a *book*, but a *sober* boy like me *cannot* help loving roast *turkey*."

"A *sober* boy, I should think!" said Kate.

"Don't interrupt us," said Marcus; "now, what's yours, Oscar?"

"I couldn't make much out of my list," remarked Oscar, and after a moment's hesitation, he read:—

> "If I could *shoot* a rabbit, I would make *gravy* of him; and then the *girl* should serve him up with *onions*, in the most *sublime* style."

"Why, I bet I could do better than that," exclaimed Ronald.

"Stop, stop, Ronald!" cried Marcus; "where are your manners?"

"Something came into my head, just then, and I spoke before I thought," replied the impulsive boy, somewhat abashed.

"Let him try my list—I don't care if he does beat me," said Oscar, good naturedly.

"No," replied Marcus, "I think he had better not—you have done well enough yourself. Now, Kate, we will hear yours."

Kate then read:—

> "I don't care much about *poetry*, and I hate *physic*, but I *should* like to hit *Ronald* with a *broomstick*."

"You'd better try it!" cried Ronald, jumping into an attitude of self-defence, as the merry laugh rang over the house.

Sentences were also read by Marcus and Ellen Blake, who had now become an inmate of the house. Another round was then proposed with a larger list of words; and now that the character of the play was better understood, they found it even more amusing than at first.

The "Hay-Mow Debating Society," so named from the place in which it usually held its meetings, was established at the commencement of the vacation, and met once or twice a week until the new term commenced. All the children belonged to it, and all were required to take part in the discussions. Subjects were assigned beforehand, and disputants appointed for each side, so that all were prepared to say something. The questions discussed were not perhaps so important as those which sometimes agitate senates and parliaments, but they were such as the young debaters could grasp, and feel an interest in. Marcus gave out for the first discussion the proposition, "Education is of more value to a man than wealth." The manner in which this grave theme was handled, induced him to throw away his list of propositions for discussion, and to make a new set, of a very different order. Some of these were as follows: "Which is preferable, summer or winter?" "Which is pleasanter, a residence on a hill, or in a valley?" "Which is most desirable, a half holiday, Wednesday and Saturday afternoons, or a whole holiday, every Saturday?" "Who enjoy themselves most, boys or girls?" Though these may look like trivial questions, they served to wake up the ideas of the young people, and sometimes the debates became quite exciting, occasionally taking a very amusing turn.

One evening, as riddles, puzzles, etc., were in the ascendant, Ellen read the following from a scrap of paper:—

"There was a man of Adam's race,

Who had a certain dwelling place;

He had a house well covered o'er,

Where no man dwelt since nor before.

It was not built by human art,

Nor brick nor lime in any part,

Nor wood, nor rock, nor nails, nor kiln,

But curiously was wrought within.

'T was not in heaven, nor yet in hell,

Nor on the earth where mortals dwell.

Now if you know this man of fame,

Tell where he lived and what's his name."

"Jonah in the whale's belly!" promptly cried Ronald.

"Did you ever see this puzzle?" inquired Otis. "A man has a wolf, a goat and a cabbage to carry across a river. It wont do to leave the wolf and goat together, nor the goat and the cabbage, and he can carry only one at a time, the boat is so small. Now what shall he do?"

After a moment's thought, Kate gave the solution, as follows:—

"First he carried over the goat; then returned and got the cabbage; then he took back the goat, and left it, and carried over the wolf; then last of all he went and got the goat."

"Let's see who can find this one out," said Ronald. "A sea captain on a voyage had thirty passengers—fifteen Christians and fifteen Turks. A great tempest arose, and he had to throw half of them overboard. They agreed to let him place them in a circle, and throw every ninth man overboard, till only fifteen were left. He did so, and when he got through, every Christian was saved, and every Turk drowned. How did he do it?"

"That is easy enough," said Kate; and writing down the figures from one to thirty, she counted off every ninth one, and found that the Christians and Turks were arranged as follows:—

CCCC, TTTTT, CC, T, CCC, T, C, TT, CC, TTT, C, TT, CC, T.

"Let me propose the next puzzle," said Aunt Fanny. "What English word of seven letters can be so transposed as to make over fifty different words?"

No one could solve this question, and when the word "weather" was named, as the answer, the children could hardly credit the fact that it was so prolific, until they had each made out a list of words. Throwing out quite a number that were obtained by using a single letter more than once, the following long list remained, which perhaps does not exhaust the subject:—

We,	Where,	Ewe,	Tea,	Her,	Here,
Wet,	Wreath,	Ere,	Tear,	He,	Hare,

War,	Wrath,	At,	Tree,	Ha,	Heat,
Wart,	Water,	Ah,	Thaw	Hat,	Haw,
Were,	Ear,	Ate,	Tare,	Hate,	Hew,
Wear,	Eat,	Art,	Tar,	Hater,	Rat,
What,	Eater,	Awe,	There,	Hart,	Rate,
Whet,	Earth,	Are,	Three,	Heart,	Raw,
Wheat.	Ether.	The.	Taw.	Hear.	Re-wet.

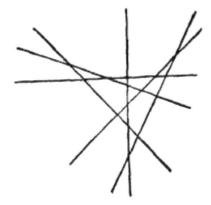

"There, I have made forty angles with only five straight lines," said Kate, holding up a slip of paper; "can any body beat that?"

"Let me try," said Marcus; and in a few minutes he pushed towards Kate the accompanying figure, remarking, "There, I've made only six lines, and if I've counted right, there are sixty angles."

While the others were amusing themselves with angles, Oscar made the annexed sketch, and now passed it to the others, giving out with it the following problem:

"A man had a piece of land exactly square, and having four trees scattered over it, as you see in the picture. The house took up one quarter of the land, and was occupied by four tenants. The owner promised them the use of the land, rent free, if they could divide it into four parts of the same size and shape, and each to have one tree. The question is, how did they do it?"

After some little puzzling of wits, the lot was divided as in the annexed illustration, and the tenants were congratulated on the good bargain they had made.

"Otis," said Ronald, "I'll bet you can't tell what the half of nine is."

"It's four and a half—any fool might know that," replied Otis.

"No it isn't," continued Ronald, "it's either four or six, just as you please, and I can prove it;" and writing IX, he folded the paper across the middle and made his promise good.

"Speaking of arithmetical puzzles," said Aunt Fanny, "I remember one that I worked over for a long time, before I could see into it. It was something like this: Two Arabs sat down to dinner, one having five loaves, and the other three. A stranger came along and asked permission to eat with them, which they granted. After the stranger had dined, he laid down eight pieces of money and departed. The owner of the five loaves took five pieces, and left three for the other, who thought he had not received his share. So they went to a magistrate, and he ordered that the owner of the five loaves should have *seven* pieces of the money, and the other only one. Was this just?"

"Why, no, it's plain enough that it wasn't," said Otis. "Each man ought to have as many pieces of money as he had loaves."

"Yes, it was just," continued Aunt Fanny; "otherwise you would pay the man of three loaves for the bread he ate himself. To prove this, divide each loaf into three equal parts, making in all twenty-four parts, and take it for granted that each person ate an equal or one-third part of the whole. You will find that the stranger had seven parts of the person who contributed five loaves or fifteen parts, and only one of him who contributed three loaves, or nine parts."

"O yes, I see into it, now," said Otis.

"That reminds me," said Marcus, "of an anecdote that I read in a newspaper the other day. I treasured it up, intending to relate it in school some day, to illustrate the importance of understanding arithmetic. It seems two carpenters took a job for one hundred and fifty dollars. One of them, whom we will call A, worked one day more than the other, B. The wages of a carpenter were two dollars per day. When the work was finished, they divided the money, each taking seventy-five dollars. Then A wished B to give him two dollars more for the extra day, but B refused, as he saw that if he did so, A would have four dollars more than he, which was evidently unjust. A insisted, and B insisted, and finally they quarrelled. Some of the bystanders took the part of A, and some of B; and yet the paper adds that all the parties were Americans, and had attended the common schools six or eight years, where I suppose they studied arithmetic, just as I suppose a good many other children do, without troubling themselves to understand it."

"How should you have settled that dispute, Otis?" inquired Mrs. Page.

"I should have told them to give A two dollars for his extra day, and divide the rest equally," replied Otis.

"Or if B had given A one dollar, it would have amounted to the same thing," said Mrs. Page.

"Your story," said Aunt Fanny, "reminds me of an anecdote of a very rich miser who lived in England, in the time of Cromwell. His name was Audley. He had a wonderful knack of getting and keeping money, and was not at all particular how he obtained it, if he did not make himself liable to the law. He once heard of a poor tradesman who had been sued by a merchant for two hundred pounds. The debtor could not meet the demand, and was declared insolvent. Audley then went to the merchant, and offered him forty pounds for the debt, which was gladly accepted. He next went to the tradesman, and offered to release him from the debt for fifty pounds, on condition that he would enter into a bond to pay for the accommodation. The debtor was delighted with the offer, especially as the terms of the bond were so easy. He was only required to pay to Audley, sometime within twenty years of that time, one penny progressively doubled, on the first day of twenty consecutive months; and in case he failed to fulfil these easy terms, he was to forfeit five hundred pounds. Thus relieved of his debt, he again commenced business, and flourished more than ever. Two or three years after, Audley walked into his shop one morning, and demanded his first payment. The tradesman paid him his penny, and thanked him for the favor he had done him. On the first day of the next month, Audley again called, and received his two pence; a month later, he received four pence; and so on for several months, doubling the sum each time. But at last the tradesman's suspicions were aroused, and he entered into a calculation of his subsequent payments. I do not remember the sum which it amounted to—"

"Wait a minute—let me figure it up," interrupted Kate, and she at once set her pencil in motion. The calculation employed her and the others several minutes. It was ascertained that the tradesman's last payment would have amounted to two thousand one hundred and eighty-six pounds, and that the total sum of all the payments would have been four thousand three hundred and sixty-nine pounds, omitting odd shillings and pence!

"I suppose the man paid the forfeit, when he found that out," said Ellen.

"Yes, he paid the miser five hundred pounds for his kindness," replied Aunt Fanny.

"I don't see how any one can dislike arithmetic—I think it is a very interesting study," remarked Kate.

"How curious it is about the figure 9," said Oscar; "you may multiply any number you please by 9, and the figures in the product, added together, will make 9, or a series of 9's. As—

9

7

—

63—6 + 3 = 9

9

3

—

27—2 + 7 = 9

9

12

——

108—1 + 8 = 9

and so on with any number, no matter how large."

"You can do the same with any of the multiples of 9," said Aunt Fanny, "as 18, 27, 36, 45, 54, etc. If you multiply these by any number whatever, you will have a series of 9's in the product. Try it."

Several experiments were made, with such results as the following:

46

18

————

828—8 + 2 + 8 = 18—1 + 8 = 9

117

27

————

3159—3 + 1 + 5 + 9 = 18—1 + 8 = 9

"There is another thing about the figure 9 very curious," said Marcus. "If you take any number composed of two figures, reverse it, and subtract the smaller from the larger, the sum of the figures in the answer will always be 9."

This was found to be true, as in the following examples:

96

69

——

27—2 + 7 = 9

54

45

——

9

84

48

——

36—3 + 6 = 9

98

89

—

9

Marcus then explained that numbers composed of three or more figures, transposed and subtracted in the same way, would always give a series of 9's in the product. The children tried the experiment, and the following are some of their examples:

723

237

—-

486—4 + 8 + 6 = 18

8962

2698

——

6264—6 + 2 + 6 + 4 = 18

32189

28913

——-

3276—3 + 2 + 7 + 6 = 18

863577

736578

———

126999 = four 9's

9216358

1982536

———-

7233822 = three 9's

"That *is* curious; but why is it so—does anybody know?" inquired Ronald.

"It will take a wiser head than mine to tell why it is so," replied Marcus.

"I found out something the other day about figures that I didn't know before," remarked Ronald; "and that is, that if you wish to multiply a number by five, you can get the same result by dividing by 2, and adding a 0 if there is no remainder, or 5 if there is a remainder. Thus, 5 times 12 are 60. Divide 12 by 2, and add a 0, and you get 60. Or 5 times 83 are 415; divide 83 by 2, and add 5, because there is a remainder, and you have the same number, 415."

"That is quite a convenient process, sometimes," said Miss Lee, "but there is no mystery about it, like the properties of the figure 9. It is in fact the same thing as multiplying by 10 and dividing by 2."

"So it is," replied Ronald. "Well, it's queer that I didn't find that out myself— I thought that I had discovered something new."

"Do you know how to make the magic square, Marcus?" inquired Otis.

"I used to know how to make *a* magic square, for there are several hundreds of them," replied Marcus. "Let me see if I can do it, now—I suppose I have forgotten all about it."

"What is a magic square?" inquired Ellen.

"It is a table of figures that can be added together in a great many different ways with the same result," replied Miss Lee.

Marcus in a few minutes produced the simplest form of the magic square; and turning to a book in the library, he found another one, both of which are here given:

4	9	2
3	5	7
8	1	6

1	16	11	6
13	4	7	10
8	9	14	3
12	5	2	15

The several columns in these tables may be added up in the usual way, or crosswise, or diagonally (from one angle to its opposite) and the result will always be the same—15 in the first, and 34 in the second square.

Such were some of the methods by which the children were amused, at Mrs. Page's, during the long evenings and stormy days of their vacation. They also had singing, reading aloud, story telling, and newspaper publishing, by way of change. Of this last I must tell you more.

CHAPTER XII.

THE NEWSPAPER.

AND what about the newspaper? Well, it was a famous thing, for a time, and made a great stir in the family. The idea originated with Kate, who thought it would be rare sport to edit and publish a newspaper among themselves; and as the others readily fell in with her plan, the enterprise was soon under way. Aunt Fanny, who had frequently written for the press, consented to act as editor, and Marcus and the children all agreed to contribute their portion towards sustaining the paper. The preliminaries were soon settled. The paper was to be called "THE HOME WREATH." It was to be issued weekly, and composed of one or more sheets of letter paper, according to the quantity of matter furnished. Its contents were to consist of short selections, cut from other papers, and original articles. The latter were to be written on one side of narrow slips of paper, of a uniform size, so that, with the selections, they could be readily pasted into their places, in columns. Of course, but one copy of each paper could be prepared, which was to circulate as common property. The editor was authorized to reject, correct or condense whatever was sent for publication. Communications were to be sent to her through the letter-box; and it was further agreed that those who contributed an article or letter to the "Wreath" every week, should be exempted from further duties as members of the "Letter-writing Society," if they did not choose to keep up their private correspondence.

The appearance of the first number of the "Home Wreath" was quite an event in the household. The editor maintained a dignified reserve in regard to its contents, until the day of publication, when it was quietly ushered before its little public, six or seven pairs of eyes being intently fastened upon it, before it had been two minutes from "the office." As one and another, who had "a finger in the pie," recognized their bantlings in the crowded columns, they looked pleased and surprised, while others, who searched in vain for their contributions, seemed still more surprised, and not quite so well pleased. But here are the "Notices to Correspondents," which doubtless explain it all. Ah, yes, the editor is already bothered with articles too long for her little paper, or too carelessly written to appear in its columns. Well, perhaps this will be a salutary warning to the offenders; and meanwhile, they can avenge themselves by criticising the articles which have been more successful than their own. But we hear no captious criticism, and perceive no signs of ill nature. The "Wreath" is read, laughed over, discussed and admired by all, and at once takes its place as an "established fact."

The second number of the new paper promptly appeared, the next week, and was generally regarded as an improvement on the first. The third was indeed a surprise number, and produced a great sensation in the family. It was issued on Ronald's birth-day, who went early to the letter-box, thinking himself entitled to the remembrance of his correspondents, on such an occasion. He found a lot of small packages in the box, addressed to different persons, on one of which he found his own name. Tearing off the envelope, there appeared before him the "Home Wreath," neatly printed from real type, on printing paper! He could scarcely credit his eyes, at first, but the evidence of its genuineness was too plain to be disputed, for there was one of his own articles in real print! The discovery was quickly known all over the house, and each of the inmates found a copy of the paper in the post office, bearing his or her address. Marcus and the editor both feigned surprise, when questioned about the affair; but after a while the facts leaked out. An old playmate and intimate friend of Marcus was employed in the printing office of the neighboring village. Marcus frequently visited him, and, with a view of getting up a birth-day present for Ronald, arranged with his friend to print the "Wreath" for that occasion. The plan was successfully carried out, as we have seen.

A transcript of this little sheet is given on the next two leaves, somewhat reduced in its dimensions and the size of its type, to suit our pages, but containing all the matter of the original.

THE HOME WREATH.

===

VOL. I.   HIGHBURG, DECEMBER 4.   No. 3.

===

THE HOME WREATH:

A Weekly Journal for Home Improvement.

PAGE & CO., PUBLISHERS.

Terms—Gratis.

For the Home Wreath,

LINES,

INSCRIBED TO RONALD D. PAGE.

I'm twelve! I'm twelve to-day!

Hurrah, boys! let us shout!

Come, leave your work and play,

And kick old care away;

Ye gloomy thoughts, get out!

We'll have no mopes about—

I'm twelve! I'm twelve to-day!

I'm twelve! I'm twelve to-day!

A dozen years have fled

Since first the morning ray,

All sober, cold and gray,

Stole in upon my head;

How fast old Time hath sped!

I'm twelve! I'm twelve to-day!

I'm twelve! I'm twelve to-day!

Then help me to be glad!

Come all, and let's be gay—

There's nothing more to pay

For being bright than sad;

Cheer up, then, lass and lad!

I'm twelve! I'm twelve to-day!

An Exercise for Scholars.

IN England, young candidates for appointment in the civil service are subjected to rigid examinations, designed to test their abilities and acquirements. The following extract, which we have somewhat abridged, shows one of the methods adopted for securing this end. It is said to be a literal copy of a document which a young applicant for a government clerkship was required to correct while undergoing his examination. We wonder how many of our young readers could put it into proper shape without consulting the dictionary.—ED.

"CHARACTER OF WASHINGTON.—At the braking out of the revolushonery war in Amerrica, Washinton joined the caus of indipendance. To detale his conduct in the yeares which followed would be butt to relaite the hystery of the American War. It may be said generaly that wethin a verry short peeriod after the declarashion of indipendance the affairs of Amerrica were in a condishun so desparate, that perhapps nothing but the piculear caractar of Washinton's genious could have retreaved them. It required the consumate prudance, the calm whisdom, the inflexable firmness, the modarate and well-balenced temper of Washinton to imbrace such a plann of pollicy and to pursivere in it: to resist the tempations of entreprize to fix the confidance of his solders without the attraction of victory: to support the spirrit of the armey and the peopel ammidst those sloe and caushious planns of difensive warfare wich are more despereting than defeate itself: to restrain his owne hambition and the empettuosity of his troupes: to indure temparary hobscurety for the sallvation of his contry and for the attanement of solled and imortal glory: and to suffer even temparary reproach and oblaquy, supported by the haprobation of his own consience, and the applaus of that small number of wise men whose praise is an earnest of the hadmeration and grattitoode of possterity. Corage is enspired by succes, and it may be stimulated to dasperate exirtion even by callamity, but is generally pallseyed by inactivity. A sestem of caushous defence is the severest tryal of human fortitoode and by this teste the firmness of Washington was tryde."

***

HATE.—Hannah More said: "If I wanted to punish an enemy, it should be by fastening on him the trouble of constantly hating somebody."

The Home Wreath.

***

SATURDAY, DECEMBER 4.

***

Nothing Insignificant.

OUR humble sheet is a very small affair; but if any stern critic is disposed to despise it on that account, let us remind him that there is nothing so small as to be wholly insignificant, when viewed in all its relations. We everywhere find little things linked with greater, and thousands of minute and hidden causes are constantly interlocking and working together, to bring about those events which impress us with their vastness and importance. A spark of fire may set in train a conflagration which will lay waste thousands of acres. Large and populous islands in the Pacific Ocean owe their origin to very small insects. The great globe itself is made up of little particles—the universe is but an aggregate of atoms. The astronomer finds it necessary to note the minutest fractions of time in observing the transit of a star whose age is perhaps measured by thousands of centuries, and whose revolutions extend through infinite space. Thus are moments linked with ages in the economy of nature, and thus are we reminded that nothing is so minute as to be insignificant.

I Can't.

This phrase is always in the mouth of some children when requested to do anything. We once knew a boy who was greatly addicted to its use. He wanted to learn to skate, but after one unsuccessful attempt, he gave it up, saying, "I can't." The next summer several of his playmates learned to swim, and he also wanted to learn; but after getting his mouth and ears full of water, one day, he cried, "I can't," and that was the end of his swimming experiments. If his class had a difficult lesson, he never learned it, and his excuse was always the same—"I can't." We once set him a copy in his writing-book, and told him that if he could not imitate it perfectly, he must write as well as he could. "I can't," was the ready reply. "What!" we exclaimed, "*can't* you write as well as you can?" He looked ashamed, but made no reply.

That boy is now a young man, but he is an ignorant, idle, and shiftless fellow, and, we fear, will never be of much use either to himself or to the world.

Commend us to the boy or girl who never says "I can't," except when enticed to do wrong. "I can" does all things; "I can't," nothing.

To Correspondents.

Several articles intended for this number are crowded out. We shall probably have to issue a double number next week, to accommodate our friends.

We observe that some of our correspondents occasionally apply the pronoun *thou*, and the pronominal adjectives *thy* and *thine*, to plural nouns. This is wrong. *You* and *yours* may be used either in the singular or plural number; but *thou*, *thy* and *thine* are always singular. You cannot say to a father and mother, as a poem which we lately saw in a newspaper, (*not* the "Wreath,") said,—

"*Thy* darling is in heaven."

News Items.

☞ The Winter Term of the Highburg Academy commences on Monday next, and will continue eleven weeks. Robert Upton, A. M., Preceptor; Mr. Marcus Page, Assistant Teacher; and Miss Martha D. Tillotson, Teacher of Drawing and Music.

☞ It is reported that traces of bears have been recently seen near Turkey Hill, in the eastern part of Highburg. Several bears have been killed this winter in the upper part of the county, and we should not be surprised if some of the "varmints" made us a visit ere long.

☞ A lynx was shot last week in Burlington. The paper from which we glean this item says: "The animal is a rare one in Vermont. It is of a grayish color, with ears ending in tufts of black hair, standing [not the 'ears,' nor the 'hair,' we presume, but the lynx] a little more than a foot high, and measuring three feet in length. It subsists on hares, rabbits, and such small animals, occasionally attacking a sheep, or even a deer, by dropping on them [it] from a branch of a tree."

☞ Two boys who had been skating in New York, a week or two since, were attacked with violent cramps and inflammation, and one of them died from the effects. It is conjectured that they laid down upon the ice, while heated from their exercise. This should be a warning to skaters.

☞ The snow which fell Wednesday, though light, is sufficient to make pretty good sleighing, and every body seems to be improving it. The proprietors, contributors and subscribers of the "Wreath" took their first sleigh-ride, this season, on Thursday. They were all comfortably stowed away in a sleigh and a pung!

Correspondence.

For the Wreath.

Small Beginnings.

A gentleman was once examining a very large and fine library in Boston, when the lady who had introduced him, asked him if he would like to see the "nucleus" of the collection. (If you do not know what "nucleus" means, you will have to turn to the dictionary, as I can think of no simpler word to substitute for it.) "Yes, I should like to see it," replied the visitor. She then exhibited to him a Latin dictionary, which she said was purchased by the owner when a boy, with money obtained by the sale of blueberries. The owner was a farmer's boy, and that is the way he began his fine library. He is now a learned man, and is well known in this country and in Europe.

For the Wreath.

Vanity—A Fable.

Two birds, whose plumage was very brilliant, and whose song was beautiful, were sitting on a tree, singing, when they discovered a man looking at them very intently. "There is an admirer—see how we have entranced him!" cried one of the birds, and she put on her proudest air, and warbled her sweetest song. "I do not like to be gazed at so earnestly by a stranger," modestly replied the other bird; "come, let us go and hide ourselves from the intruder." The modest bird flew into a thicket and concealed herself; but the other, flying to the top-most bough, began to show off all her airs, when suddenly the sharp crack of a gun was heard, and the silly bird fell dead.

MORAL.—"Pride goeth before destruction, and an haughty spirit before a fall."

KETA.

For the Wreath.

MISS EDITOR:—I feel slighted. You are all writing for the "Wreath," but not a soul of you has asked me to contribute to your interesting paper. Why is this? Have I not heard some of you say that I know as much as many human bipeds of the same age? Don't I understand almost everything that you say to me? And if I only *could* talk, wouldn't I rattle away as fast as any of you? I bet I would. If I don't talk, it isn't because I've got no ideas, depend on that. But you see I can write, although perhaps you did not know it. But fearing I am an intruder, I will stop.

ROVER.

For the Wreath.

The Snow.

Hurrah! The snow has come!—Now wont we have fine times! I like to see it come thick and fast, and bury everything up. How curious it is, to see the woods, and fences, and stones, and roofs, and fields, and hills, covered over with the pure white snow! What fun it is to roll and tumble in it! I like to have the roads all blocked up, so that we can't get anywhere, not even to school. Then what fun it is to break out the ways! We have a large sled, with a plough lashed to the off side. Then we hitch on six or eight yoke of oxen, and are ready for a start. The boys load up the sled, and a lot of men go ahead to shovel through the deep drifts, and so we go all over town till the roads are broken out.

RON.

For the Wreath.

A Cunning Fellow.

The summer that I lived in Brookdale, I was one day in the woods, with my cousin Jerry, and another boy, named Clinton, when we found a fox's hole. We began to dig her out; but when we got to the end of the hole, we found nothing. Clinton said he had known a fox to bank herself up in a separate cell, when her hole was invaded; and we determined to see if our fox had not served us so. We dug, and soon found eight little ones, all stowed away in a cell by themselves. We then tried to find the old one, but could not. So we took the little ones and started off; but on looking back we saw the old fox dart out of the hole and disappear. We went back to examine the hole again, and found that she had a separate cell for herself, which escaped our search. So she saved her own life, but she lost her little ones.

OSCAR.

Gleanings.

Digest what you read. It is not what you eat but what you digest that gives nourishment to the body; so with the mind. Young people sometimes run through a book, and are not able to tell afterwards what they have been reading.

"John," said the schoolmaster, "you will soon be a man, and will have to do business. What do you suppose you will do when you have to write letters, unless you learn to spell, better?" "O, sir, I shall put easy words in them."

"Dick, I say, why don't you turn the buffalo robe t'other side out?—hair is the warmest."

"Bah, Tom, you get out. Do you suppose the animal himself didn't know how to wear his hide?"

CHAPTER XIII.

MASTER PAGE.

SO impatient was Ronald to enter upon his academic career, that he had his school books and his slate all ready for a start, Saturday afternoon. On going up to his chamber, later in the day, he was pleasantly surprised to find a nice new satchel upon his table, which his mother had made for him, as a birth-day present. He packed his books into it, and swung it over his shoulder, and walked back and forth, to see how it would seem. While he was thus indulging in pleasant anticipations, his room-mate, Otis, was undergoing a very different experience. Entering the chamber, without noticing Ronald, he threw himself upon the bed, and burst into tears. Ronald did not need to inquire what ailed him. His parents had that afternoon made their promised visit to Kate and Otis, and had just started for home, and the poor boy was consequently suffering from that most distressing malady of the mind— home-sickness. Ronald's efforts to enliven him proved unavailing, and he was reluctantly compelled to leave him to his grief, which did not wholly subside until sleep came to his relief.

On Monday morning, more than half an hour before the first stroke of the academy bell was heard, Ronald was busily engaged in hurrying up his academical associates, whose moderation in getting themselves ready for the day's business seemed to him almost too bad to be patiently endured.

However, contrary to his predictions, all arrived at the academy in good season, though they went in straggling parties—for it was the preference of all to walk, rather than ride, when the weather and the roads permitted. Of course, they carried their dinners.

At five minutes before nine o'clock the bell sounded, and the scholars and teachers assembled in the school-room. The forenoon was spent in taking the names of the pupils, assigning seats, forming classes, giving out lessons, and in general remarks to the students on the purpose for which they had assembled, and the duties which they were expected to perform. Most of the preliminary matters were settled, in the forenoon, and the regular studies commenced with the afternoon session.

The incidents of the day afforded plenty of topics for conversation to Marcus and the students from his family, as they proceeded home, at night. General satisfaction was expressed that one of the monitors' desks, overlooking a division of the smaller boys, had been assigned to Oscar. This arrangement seemed peculiarly gratifying to Ronald and Otis, who thus came under his oversight, and who smiled incredulously, when he declared that he should keep a particularly sharp eye upon them. Oscar expressed himself as much pleased with the preceptor, Mr. Upton. Kate, who had been promoted to the highest class, and was in excellent spirits, said she always admired Mr. Upton, and thought she should rather like his new assistant, Mr. Page. Otis and Ronald, on the other hand, were a little disappointed because Marcus had disregarded their joint request, that they might sit together, and had placed them so far apart that any intercourse during school hours, except by means of winks, signs and paper "spit balls," would be out of the question. The reason Marcus gave for this refusal,— the fear that they would have too good a time together,—was not very consoling to the boys. Instead of Otis, Ronald had for his nearest comrade the boy who blotted his writing-book at the district school, Lewis Daniels. Both Marcus and Ronald, however, treated Lewis with kindness, and tried to make him forget the injury he had inflicted upon the latter.

The ardor with which Ronald set out for school in the morning was a little dampened by one or two other incidents that occurred during the day. At noon, as he approached a group of large boys, he heard one of them say—

"I don't care for Marcus Page—he's nothing but a boy, himself. He was a scholar, here, for a year or more after I joined the academy."

On turning round, and seeing Ronald near, the large boy added—

"Here, you youngster, you needn't go and tell Page everything you hear, because you happen to live with him; because if you do, you'll be sorry for it."

Ronald had no heart to report this conversation to Marcus, though he cared nothing for the threat. His ears tingled, however, to hear Marcus spoken of in this way, and from that moment he felt a strong dislike towards the boy in question, who, to do him justice, was not so bad as he seemed, but only had an unhappy habit of saying more than he felt, and threatening more than he was willing to perform.

Another large boy,—a mischievous but not ill-meaning fellow,—annoyed Ronald a good deal by applying to him the nickname *Frenchy*, and telling him he had got to wear it as his "academical name." Ronald reported this to Marcus; but the latter advised him to take no notice of the affair, telling him that the inventor of the nickname would probably soon forget all about it, if he saw that it did not trouble Ronald.

"Who would have thought of seeing Jessie Hapley in the academy!" exclaimed Kate, as they were walking home. "I declare, I never was more surprised in my life—they are so poor, you know."

"But Jessie is a very fine girl, if she is poor," said Marcus.

"O, yes, I like her very much," promptly responded Kate; "and I'm glad she is going to school with us; but I didn't suppose her father could afford to send her."

"She earned the money herself, to pay for her tuition," added Marcus. "She sees she has got to support herself, if not the rest of the family, and she is anxious to qualify herself for teaching. She thinks she is better adapted to that business than to any other, and I think so, too. She is an excellent scholar, and you will have to look out for your laurels, Kate, now that she is in school."

"Well, she is older than I am," said Kate, quite unconcerned.

"Only a few months," added Marcus; "besides, her school privileges have been very limited, compared with yours."

"No matter, I don't think I shall be jealous of her," replied Kate. "I always did like Jessie, and if any girl is going to excel me, I'd rather it should be her than any one else. But Abby Leonard declares that she wont associate with her. She says she hates to see a poor girl all the time 'trying to be somebody.'"

"I am afraid Abby is not so wise as she might be, if she *has* enjoyed the advantages of city society," observed Marcus.

"Do you know what she does to make herself look pale and slender?" inquired Kate. "She eats chalk, and slate pencils, and drinks lots of vinegar.

She advised me to try it, because I'm so plump. She thinks it doesn't look interesting and genteel, to be fat."

"I hope you wont follow her advice, unless you wish to ruin your health," replied Marcus. "I shall have to speak to her about this subject—she has fallen into a very dangerous practice, as well as a foolish theory. In fact, if she consumes those articles to any extent, she is committing suicide, whether she knows it or not."

The current of events continued to flow on smoothly day after day, at the academy, until one morning, when the principal failed to appear. Marcus opened the session, at the usual hour, and soon after received a note from Mr. Upton, stating that he was ill, and unable to be present. Marcus conducted the school through the day, with very good success, and before returning home, called upon his associate, whom he found prostrated with an illness which would probably detain him from his labors for several weeks.

"I do not see but that you will have to take my place, for a week or two, Marcus," said Mr. Upton. "We have got well under way, and everything is going on smoothly, so that I think you and Miss Tillotson can manage matters very well, for a little while."

Marcus shook his head, and looked somewhat alarmed, at this proposition. Nor was he slow in making known his objections. He had had little experience in teaching, even the simpler branches, and as to the higher studies, he was appalled by what he considered his lack of qualifications. Then how could he, an inexperienced youth, maintain the discipline of such a school, composed in part of pupils as old as himself, some of whom had been his school-mates a year previous? Mr. Upton, however, did not give much heed to these objections. He did not doubt Marcus's qualifications to teach any of the branches, and as to the discipline, if he experienced any trouble, the trustees would give him all necessary aid. As it would be impracticable to make any other arrangement, at least for a week or two, Marcus at length consented to assume this new responsibility.

The next morning, Marcus informed the scholars of the new duties that had devolved upon him, and expressed his determination to do his best to make good their preceptor's place, at the same time soliciting their aid and co-operation in the work. With now and then a trifling exception, the school was as orderly and quiet as usual, and Marcus was soon satisfied that the public sentiment of his charge was on his side, and would sustain him in his position. This was especially true of the older scholars, of whom he had most stood in doubt. Appreciating the value of their privileges, even the least sedate of them had no inclination to come in collision with their young teacher, for whom, indeed, they all felt some degree of esteem, as a personal friend. Neither did the younger pupils manifest any disposition to question his authority. Two days' experience satisfied Marcus that the only pupils from whom he had reason to anticipate trouble were three or four boys, some thirteen or fourteen years old; and he had no doubt that he should be able to bring these turbulent spirits into subjection, in a few days.

These troublesome boys happened to be seated together, near the back part of the room, and at times they created some little disturbance in that quarter. Before dismissing school at night, Marcus pleasantly informed them, separately, that he proposed to re-seat some of the boys, and then proceeded to arrange such an exchange of desks as brought them nearer to his platform, and at the same time scattered them apart. One or two of the worst of them, by this change, were brought under the monitorial eye of Oscar.

Marcus now made it a special object to secure the confidence and good-will of the more unruly part of his charge. One noon, he saw several of his most troublesome boys at work upon a snow figure, in the grove back of the academy. He approached them, and, commending their skilful workmanship, soon drew them into a pleasant conversation. As he watched the growing statue, he observed that the credit belonged mainly to one of the lads, named Charles Wilder, who directed the labor of the others. Marcus had noticed that this boy exercised a good deal of influence over his comrades; but in the school-room he was rather inattentive to his lessons, and inclined to mischief.

"Charlie's the boy for this kind of work," said one of the lads, addressing Marcus.

"Yes, I see he understands it," replied Marcus. "You have quite an artist's eye, Charlie. Where did you learn so much about modelling?"

"O, I don't know much about it—all I do know came natural to me," replied the boy.

"I remember seeing an account of a young man in this State," said Marcus, "who made a statue of snow and ice that was so beautiful, that a rich gentleman ordered a copy of it in marble. Perhaps you will be as fortunate as he, one of these days."

"I mean to be a sculptor, some time or other," replied Charles, his face lighting up with an expressive smile.

"I suppose it's hard work to make a statue, isn't it?" inquired one of the boys.

"No, I don't know as it is exactly what you would call hard work, but it requires a good deal of skill, and taste, and genius, to make a fine statue," replied Marcus.

"O, I suppose they have plenty of tools, and pound it out," observed another boy.

"Pound out your grandma'am with tools, just as much!" exclaimed Charles, with a glance of mingled pity and indignation at the boy who held this degraded view of the beautiful art to which his soul was thus early wedded.

"You must be somewhat proficient in drawing, Charlie, to design such a statue as this," resumed Marcus.

"I'm very fond of drawing, but I don't know much about it," replied Charles.

"You are not taking lessons in drawing, I believe?" inquired Marcus.

"No, sir; I wanted to, but father said it was of no use," replied Charles.

"I think it *would* be of use," said Marcus; "that is, if you have as much taste for it as I think you have. I wish you would let me see one of your drawings,—perhaps I could persuade your father to let you take lessons, if I think it worth while."

"I've got one in my desk—I'll run and get it," said Charles; and he darted off, soon returning with a very neatly executed drawing of a dog hunting a stag, which he had copied with much skill from an engraving.

"That is very creditable to you—very much so," said Marcus, as he examined the picture. "You certainly have a taste for drawing, and your father must let you take lessons of Miss Tillotson. I will speak to him about it, this week."

The young artist looked pleased and grateful, and Marcus left him, not only feeling a new interest in the boy, but with a firm persuasion that he should have no further trouble with him.

The above is a representation of Charles's drawing. Marcus took the trouble to call upon Mr. Wilder, that afternoon, and after a little persuasion obtained permission for Charles to take drawing lessons.

A day or two after this, Marcus found on his desk, one morning, an anonymous note, which read as follows:—

> "TO MASTER PAGE:—I think it is too bad that some of the scholars should be allowed to have keys to their arithmetics, when it is against the rules. Fair play is a jewel. This is from
>
> ONE WHO KNOWS."

Marcus was for a time in doubt what to do in relation to this complaint. The anonymous character of the note deprived it of all claim upon his attention; and its apparently implied censure upon him for something of which he had no knowledge, rendered it still more objectionable. After reflection, however, he determined to investigate the matter at once, leaving to a future occasion some remarks to the school on the impropriety and meanness of writing anonymous letters of complaint. He accordingly remarked to the school:—

"I have been informed that some of the scholars have keys to their arithmetics. I wish all such would rise."

Much to his surprise, Oscar promptly arose, and said:—

"I have a key, but I have made no improper use of it. I do all my sums before I look at the answers."

"Did you not know that it is contrary to the rules for any scholar to have a key?" said Marcus.

"Yes, sir," replied Oscar.

"That is sufficient," said Marcus. "You have violated one of our rules, whatever use you may have made of the key. If you have it here, you may deliver it up."

Oscar obeyed the order, his appearance indicating that he felt the mild rebuke rather keenly. It is due to him to say, that with this exception, his conduct in school had thus far been quite exemplary, and his progress in his studies commendable.

After Ronald had become somewhat familiar with the school, he found it rather difficult to wholly repress the promptings to fun within him. During the first week of the principal's absence, Marcus had occasion to reprove him several times, privately, for offences of this kind, and on one occasion, detained him after school, as a punishment. One afternoon, as Marcus was hearing a class recite, he was startled by one of his most quiet boys crying out:—

"You quit that!"

"What is the matter, Edmund?" inquired Marcus.

The boy, coloring deeply replied:—

"Ronald has been snapping nut-shells at me for half an hour, and he just hit me in the eye with one. I was very busy ciphering, and I spoke before I thought. I forgot I was in school."

Ronald was called out, a handful of nuts was transferred from his pocket to the teacher's desk, and he was then directed to stand upon the platform facing the school, until he had committed to memory a page from a geography used by another class. In all this Marcus was as calm and mild as usual; but nevertheless, Ronald did not feel very pleasantly, as he took his position and commenced his task, though the punishment was not what he feared it would be, when called out. His mortification was not a little increased, when, after reciting the task, Marcus assigned him a new seat, directly under his own eye. Ronald avoided all company, on his way home, that afternoon, and seemed especially anxious to keep out of the reach of Marcus, through the rest of the day. Marcus, however, had something to say to Ronald, and after tea he found an opportunity to say it.

"Ronald," he said, "I have been thinking that I had better increase your lessons a little. I am afraid you are getting along too easily at school."

"Why, I think our lessons are pretty hard," replied Ronald, somewhat surprised.

"They are hard enough for most of your class, but you learn so readily that I shall have to give you some extra tasks," added Marcus.

"I don't think that is fair," replied Ronald. "If I get all the lessons that the others do, I should think that is enough."

"If your lessons are so easy that you learn them without much effort," continued Marcus, "you are missing the real end of going to school. It is not the chief aim of education to give a child a smattering of knowledge, but the object should be to discipline his mind, and that cannot be done without real tasks—lessons that will make him study hard, and think closely. He needs something to rouse him to exertion, and then he will begin to find out what his powers are. I think I shall let you study book-keeping and algebra, with the third class, in addition to your other lessons."

"Well, if you think best, I will try it," said Ronald.

"I have another reason for this," added Marcus. "You have too many idle moments, now. Your lessons are not hard enough to keep you out of mischief. I shall have to increase them until you have no time for idleness or mischief during study hours."

Marcus imposed the additional studies upon Ronald, the next day. The salutary effects of this, and of the incidents of the previous afternoon, were soon apparent. He was careful, however, not to overtask the boy's powers, which would have been a greater evil than the opposite error.

With Otis, Marcus found a different course of management necessary. He was more quiet and orderly in school than Ronald, but less perfect in his lessons. Indeed, he was not remarkably fond of study, and needed a little spurring, now and then, to prevent his falling below the average of his class. One afternoon, as he was walking home with Marcus, he said:—

"I can't get that sixth sum right, any way. I've tried it half a dozen times, and I get it exactly the same every time. The answer in the book must be wrong, for I know I did it right. I did the other sums in just the same way, and they came right."

"You are wrong," replied Marcus, "for I happen to know that the answer in the book is right. Georgianna Ellis came to me this afternoon with the same story. She thought the answer in the book was a mistake. But I did the sum, and found it right."

"How did you do it?" inquired Otis.

"That is for you to find out yourself, if you can," replied Marcus, with a significant accent upon the last clause of the sentence.

"Didn't you show Georgianna how to do it?" inquired Otis.

"No," replied Marcus; "I told her to read over the question carefully, and then to keep trying upon it until she got the right solution."

"Did she get it?" inquired Otis.

"I do not know," replied Marcus; "but if she has not found out her error, I have no doubt she will."

"Then I suppose you think I can do the sum, if I keep trying," said Otis.

"I have some doubts about that," replied Marcus. "I suppose I ought to give you the same direction that I gave Georgianna; but I have little faith that you would be successful, after all."

"Why couldn't I find out the answer, if she can?" inquired Otis.

"There is a great difference in scholars," replied Marcus. "Some are careful, and examine everything very closely, when they meet a difficulty, while others blunder about without much thought. Some have great perseverance, and others are quickly discouraged. And then some do not seem to have much sense, or if they have, they don't exercise it."

Otis did not push his inquiries any further, and the subject was dropped. The stimulus of shame, judiciously applied, is sometimes effective when other means fail, and so it proved in this case. Otis was not discouraged by what Marcus said, but was incited by it to a new and more earnest effort. He solved the problem, unaided, and so derived more real benefit from this one puzzling question than from all the others in the day's lesson, which he performed without difficulty.

CHAPTER XIV.

THE TROUBLESOME SCHOLAR.

THERE was one boy in the academy who still caused Marcus no little anxiety. His name was Harrison Clark, and he was about fourteen years old, and large for his age. This was his first term at the academy. He was from an adjoining town, and but little was known of him, except what he himself chose to divulge. The achievement of his short life upon which he seemed to pride himself most, was a fight he had with his former teacher, a month or two before this, in which, according to his representation, he came off victor; and he had been heard to threaten a similar infliction upon Marcus, should that personage attempt to chastise him. One or two of the elder pupils were anxious that the insolence of this pert young gentleman should be checked by a sound thrashing, and they even intimated to the teacher that aid would not be wanting, in case the boy should offer serious resistance. But Marcus thought there was a more excellent way to subdue him, and determined to try it, before resorting to harsh measures.

Marcus happened one day to fall in with a townsman of Harrison, from whom he gathered all the information he could in regard to the career and character of the boy. It appeared that he had been governed with severity, both at home and at school, so far as he had been governed at all. He had steadily grown worse, however, under this discipline, and his parents, finding they could do nothing with him, had sent him away to school, as the easiest way to rid themselves of a constant trouble. They were finally led to this course, by his altercation with his teacher. Several boys, it seemed, got into a wild frolic in the school-room, one day, before the opening of the session, in the course of which Harrison threw an inkstand at another lad, by which his face and clothes were stained, and the walls, floor, and seats soiled. The teacher, after investigating the matter, ordered Harrison to hold out his hand for punishment, which he refused to do, in an insolent manner. The teacher then attempted to seize his hand, but failing in this, he tripped the boy upon the floor, and a regular scuffle ensued. Another boy, still larger than Harrison, now rushed to the assistance of the latter, and before the disgraceful affray ended, they inflicted two or three serious blows upon the teacher, and then fled. They were both arrested for assault, and after a trial before a justice, were fined, Harrison ten dollars and the other boy five, besides the cost of the trial, which was divided between them. While it must be confessed that their punishment was just, I think few will deny that the teacher also was to be blamed for the part he acted in the affray.

"Now can't you tell me something good about Harrison?" inquired Marcus, after listening to the foregoing recital. "I believe there is always some good trait in every person, however bad."

"Well," replied the other, "I'm thinking it would be rather hard to find anything very good about that chap. I don't think he's very hardened yet, but there's precious little goodness about him, I can tell you. He thinks a good deal of his mother, and that's the best thing I ever saw about him. And he ought to like her, for she's a right down good woman—only she's one of your easy, gentle sort, that oughtn't to have anything to do with such a young scapegrace as he is."

Although Harrison had made himself sufficiently troublesome in the school-room, he had thus far avoided all flagrant offences. He manifested his disposition by an air of quiet insolence and defiance, and by petty acts of annoyance, too trivial for serious notice, even could they be proved against him, which was seldom the case. It was evident, however, that he was becoming emboldened by the absence of restraints and punishments with which he had been familiar in school, and Marcus looked forward with some solicitude to the certainty of an open collision with him, which day by day seemed more imminent. Meanwhile, the attempts of Marcus to win him over by kindness were not very well rewarded. If he spoke kindly to the boy on the play-ground or at his desk, he got no pleasant word or grateful look, in return. If he tried to draw him into conversation, the responses came grudgingly in monosyllables. On Saturday, he invited Harrison to come over to pass the afternoon with him and the children; but the boy did not come; worse yet, he did not say whether he would or not; and still worse, he expressed no thanks for the invitation.

One cold morning, soon after the school opened, Marcus was somewhat annoyed by the coughing of the scholars—not a very unusual occurrence at that season. Having reduced the school to perfect silence, so that the falling of a pin might have been heard, he proceeded to say:—

"I notice that many of the scholars have rather troublesome coughs. I have a cold myself, and I suppose I could cough as hard as any of you, if I chose to. But I am not going to do it. There are two objections to coughing. One is, it is injurious. The effort required in coughing is apt to tear the delicate fibres of the lungs. Sometimes people burst blood-vessels, while coughing, and die in consequence. The other objection is, it is unpleasant to those around us, especially in a school-room, church, or other public assembly. Sometimes, I admit, it is necessary to cough; but I think most of our coughing is unnecessary. By a little attention, and a little effort of the will, we can prevent it. Now I propose that those who have colds try the experiment with me, and we will see who will hold out longest without coughing."

Marcus had no sooner closed, than Harrison fell into a violent fit of coughing, which it was evident to all was feigned. Some of the younger scholars smiled at this ill-mannered freak, but others looked daggers at its perpetrator. Marcus uttered no rebuke, but the eyes of the rogue fell before his steady, quiet, searching look.

A day or two after this, there was great excitement in the village, occasioned by the discovery that several sheep had been killed by bears, the tracks of which were found in the neighborhood of "Turkey Hill." The presence of these animals in the town had been suspected for several weeks, but this was their first attack upon the sheep-folds of the farmers. Arrangements were at once made for a grand bear hunt, the next afternoon, and all the male population, above fifteen years of age, were invited to take part in it.

Marcus found, the next morning, that most of his boys had come to school prepared to join in the hunt, either as participants or spectators. All who could, had procured guns, and as the lads and young men lounged around the academy, in groups, examining and comparing their arms, a stranger might have suspected the existence of a "school rebellion" of a really startling description. But when the bell struck, the guns were peaceably deposited in the ante-room, and the school-room assumed its usual quiet aspect. At recess several of the boys were dismissed, having brought notes from home, requesting Marcus to excuse them at that hour. Two or three others petitioned for a similar favor, but, having no authority from their parents for making the request, Marcus felt obliged to deny them. He did this the more easily, because he thought the request a needless one. The hunting party was not to rendezvous until half past twelve o'clock—half an hour after the session closed for the day, for it was Saturday. Nevertheless, Harrison Clark, who was one of the disappointed applicants, appeared to think differently; for when the boys were called in from recess, he was missing. On looking from a window, Marcus saw him standing, gun in hand, near the post office, where a crowd of men appeared to be discussing the arrangements of the day. One of the large scholars was despatched to bring the runaway back; but Harrison saw the young man approaching, and mistrusting his errand, took to his heels, and made good his escape.

At twelve o'clock the session closed, the contents of sundry little baskets and tin pails were hurriedly disposed of for the benefit of the inner man, and most of the boys, accompanied by their teacher, then proceeded to the place of rendezvous. After waiting awhile for tardy stragglers, the hunting party was found to muster over a hundred men and boys, all armed. An experienced hunter was chosen captain, a few directions were given to the men, and the line of march was then taken up for Turkey Hill, some two miles distant.

On reaching the hunting ground, the guns were loaded, and the party then proceeded to form a ring around the hill, which was a low eminence, densely wooded, and abounding with ledges. Two files of men started in opposite directions, and encircled the hill until they met, scattering themselves apart as they proceeded. Then, to test the connection of the ring in all its parts, the captain cried to his left hand man, "*Are you there?*" and he taking up the call, according to a previously arranged plan, shouted it to the man on his left, and thus it passed around, until it came back in a few moments to the leader. He then gave the order, "*Forward!*" in a similar manner; and as it ran round the line, the party began its slow march up the hill. They continued to ascend, gradually closing up the circle, until it embraced only about an acre of woods. The circle was now quite impervious to any animal, the hunters being within a few yards of each other. Only a small portion of the ring, however, was visible at any one point, owing to the trees and brush, and the inequality of the surface. Every gun was now cocked, and every eye was straining itself, to detect some sign of the presence of Bruin. Suddenly, the sharp crack of a gun was heard, followed by another, and another; and almost immediately, a large bear bounded out, towards the part of the circle where Marcus and Oscar were stationed. But ere the poor beast could reach the line, a score of bullets were buried in his body, and he fell dead. Loud and long was the shout of triumph that went up from every side; and still louder did it grow, when it was found that this was not the only trophy, but that another though much smaller bear had been shot on the opposite side of the ring, when the reports of firearms were first heard.

The two carcasses were placed on sleds, and dragged to the village by the boys. The largest bear was found to weigh about four hundred and fifty pounds, but the weight of the other was a little short of two hundred pounds. Before the people separated for their homes, the two carcasses were put up at auction, and sold for about fifteen dollars. It was voted to give the money to the owner of the sheep killed by the bears—an aged man, in needy circumstances, who looked the gratitude he could not speak, when the generous proposal was ratified by a hearty "Aye!"

On Monday morning, when Marcus read to the school the names of absentees at the previous session, and called for excuses, he came to the following entry: "Harrison Clark—left at recess." He paused a moment, and as no excuse was offered, added—

"Harrison, when school is dismissed in the afternoon, you may come to my desk."

"This *afternoon* or *forenoon*?" inquired Harrison, not at all abashed.

"I said this *afternoon*," replied Marcus, who postponed the matter until that hour, because of the limited intermission from studies at noon.

As Marcus anticipated, Harrison was going off without paying any regard to this command, in the afternoon; but when called he went back, saying by way of apology that he forgot all about the matter. When they were alone, Marcus inquired, very pleasantly—

"Well, Harrison, how did you enjoy yourself, Saturday afternoon?"

"First-rate—didn't you?" coolly replied the boy.

"Do you think you enjoyed the hunt as much as you would if you hadn't gone off at recess, contrary to my express orders?" inquired Marcus.

"Well, yes, I don't see as that made any difference," replied Harrison, looking as calm and unconcerned as though he were discussing the point with some comrade.

"I see you are inclined to be frank," continued Marcus. "I am glad of that— I like frank, open dealing in everybody, boys as well as men. Don't you?"

"Why, yes, I do," replied the boy.

"And are you willing to be perfectly frank with me, if I will be so with you, in talking over matters now?" inquired Marcus.

"Well, I can't stop long—I agreed to go somewhere, after school," replied Harrison.

"But we must attend to this business first," replied Marcus, in a decided tone. "Now if you say you will deal frankly with me, I will proceed at once."

"Well, I will," said Harrison.

"Then I will be equally frank with you, and so we shall have a fair understanding of each other," replied Marcus. "I have noticed for several weeks, especially since Mr. Upton has been sick, that you were inclined to be disrespectful towards me, and to annoy me and the school by certain little improprieties that it was difficult to prove wilful, though they certainly seemed to be so. As I know of no reason why you should wish to trouble me—for I believe I have always treated you kindly—I have taken as charitable a view of this as I could. I have tried to think that you did not mean any harm, but were only a little odd in your ways. But when you set my authority at defiance so coolly, last Saturday, I saw that something more serious than oddity was the matter. And that something has got to be met, promptly and decidedly. Now there are two ways of meeting such a spirit in a scholar. One way is, to inflict a severe and disgraceful punishment, which will serve as a warning to the other pupils, if it does not reform the guilty one. The other way is, to win him from his error by mild and kind means.

"Now, Harrison, you know very well which of these systems of government we have adopted here. You have seen no rod or ruler, since you came here, and I hope you will not, if you stay through the term. But that is by no means certain. Sometimes, when mild measures fail, Mr. Upton adopts stern ones; but he always tries kindness first. There is only one other resort, in desperate cases, and that is, to expel the offender. Now, if I have been rightly informed, the harsh system had been pretty faithfully tried upon you before you came here, had it not?"

"I should think it had—but it didn't do any good," replied Harrison.

"And now kindness has been tried, and *that* has done no good," added Marcus, with a serious look. "What more can be done? Do you think that you ought to be privileged to do as you please, while all the other scholars are required to be obedient, and orderly, and respectful? You said you would be frank with me; now will you answer me that question, honestly?"

"I suppose not," replied Harrison, rather reluctantly.

"Very well, now I wish you to answer another question, as frankly as you did that," continued Marcus. "Do you think I ought to be expected to sacrifice my feelings, and strength, and time, in trying harsh measures upon a boy, when the experiment has already been made by others, and, as he admits, without any good result?"

"No, sir," replied the boy, in a more respectful tone than usual.

"Neither do I," said Marcus. "Then if kind measures fail, as they have in your case, so far, expulsion is the only remedy left; and that, of itself, is a very harsh, and painful, and disgraceful punishment. I can't bear to think of it. It is casting the boy out from influences that might save him, into a world of new temptations and dangers. If he were the only one involved, I would put up with a great many provocations, before I would sentence a boy to such a fate as that. But the interests of the school sometimes require that a scholar should be expelled, and then the teacher must do his duty, however painful it may be. In such a case, the teacher and the boy are not the only sufferers. The parents and friends of the offender often suffer even worse than he does. I hear, Harrison, that you have an excellent mother. Is it so?"

"Yes, sir," replied the boy.

"I have been told," continued Marcus, "that she is a very kind, gentle, and sensitive woman. I hear, also, that you appear to think a great deal of her, and I hope the report is true, for a *good* mother is a blessing for which we can never be too grateful."

The expression of the boy's face, at this mention of his mother, indicated that the report was not without foundation.

"Now," continued Marcus, "how would your mother feel, if you should go home, and tell her that you had been expelled from the academy, for misconduct? Would it not almost break her heart? For her sake, as well as yours, I hope we shall not have to fall back upon that last resort. But as I promised to be frank with you, I must tell you, in all sincerity, that the course you have been pursuing will certainly lead to expulsion, if not abandoned. I do not say this to frighten you, but I am honestly pointing out to you a *real* danger, and one that you will assuredly encounter very soon, if you do not take warning. You have been quite frank with me, so far, now I want to know if you will give me a plain and honest answer to one more question?"

"I will," replied Harrison.

"I am going to ask the question now," continued Marcus, "but you need not answer it to-night. I would rather that you should take time to think it over, and let me know your decision to-morrow. The question is this— whether you intend to keep on in your old habits, as though nothing had happened, or will you try to correct the faults I have mentioned? You will please to take notice that the question refers only to your *intentions*. I do not ask you to promise never to disobey or be disrespectful again; but if you have any intention, or even the slightest wish, to reform these habits, I want you to say so, and I will help you all I can to accomplish the work. On the other hand, if you really prefer to do as you have been doing, I want you to tell me that, just as candidly. Remember you promised to be frank. You can go, now, and to-morrow you may tell me your decision."

Harrison's bearing was somewhat more subdued and respectful than usual, when he left Marcus. The same peculiarity was apparent in his conduct the next day, in school. When school was dismissed at noon, Harrison went of his own accord to the teacher's desk, and said:—

"Mr. Page, I've thought over that matter that we talked about yesterday, and I've made up my mind to try to do better, hereafter."

"I am very glad to hear you say so, Harrison," replied Marcus, grasping the boy kindly by the hand. "If that is your intention, I have no doubt we shall get along pleasantly enough after this."

"I'm sorry I went off, Saturday, and I wont do such a thing again," added Harrison.

"That was quite a serious act of disobedience," replied Marcus, "although I have refrained from saying much about it directly, thus far. If I should conclude that the offence required some kind of punishment, notwithstanding this confession, do you feel as though you could submit to it cheerfully?"

"Yes, sir, I think I could," replied Harrison, rather hesitatingly.

"I suppose the fact that you ran away is known to all the scholars," observed Marcus. "Now should you be willing to make the apology as publicly as the offence?"

This was a pretty severe test for Harrison. Remembering the braggadocio with which he had alluded to his offence, only the day before, in the presence of many of his school-mates, it was hard to say he was willing to stand up before them all, and humbly acknowledge his fault.

"Give me a frank answer, that is all I ask," added Marcus, as he perceived the conflict in his pupil's mind.

"Well, I suppose I ought to confess in public, and I must do it, if you say so, but it will come dreadful hard," replied the boy, who seemed anxious and perplexed.

"Yes, I suppose it would be a very disagreeable duty," said Marcus; "and on the whole, I think I will not ask it of you. The scholars know that I have taken private notice of the offence, and perhaps that will answer every purpose. If you will show to them a better example hereafter, that is all I will require, this time. The past shall all be forgiven and forgotten."

The boy looked pleased and grateful, and before retiring, repeated his promise of amendment. This promise he kept. His feelings towards Marcus seemed to have undergone an entire change. True, every fault in his character and conduct was not corrected at once; but as there seemed to be a prevailing disposition in him to conform to the rules of the school, united with a sincere respect for his teacher, Marcus looked upon his errors as leniently as possible, and endeavored to encourage him in his good work by every proper method.

The next Monday, Mr. Upton resumed his post, and complimented Marcus very highly on finding the academy in so prosperous a state.

CHAPTER XV.

ABOUT SAM HAPLEY.

MR. HAPLEY, the father of Jessie and Sam, and the near neighbor of the Pages, seemed to be growing more slack than ever, this winter. Fields of corn-stalks were still standing on his farm, although it was well advanced in December, he having neglected to cut them in the fall, for his cattle. It was even reported that a good part of his potatoes were frozen into the ground, as he had delayed digging them until it was too late. His family and stock were not so well provided for that they could afford thus to throw away the produce of the farm. Plenty by no means reigned in the house, and as to the barn, its inmates bore unmistakable testimony that poor hay, with few roots and less grain, would not keep cattle in good condition.

One morning, after the last stick of cut wood had been consumed, and a rod or more of the fence, also, had been used to "keep the pot boiling," Mr. Hapley mustered sufficient resolution to go up to the wood-lot, with his team, after another load. He got a neighbor to go with him, for although one might have supposed Sam was large enough to chop wood, Mr. Hapley always said he was "good for nothing to work," and Sam was very careful never to give him occasion to alter his opinion.

In all such expeditions as this, there were two things that always accompanied Mr. Hapley. These were, a pipe and a jug. With something to smoke, and something to drink, he considered himself amply fortified against all the demands of appetite, for half a day at least. The young man who accompanied him on this occasion, was not at all averse to an occasional mug of cider, or whiskey, or, indeed to any other beverage that could claim kindred to these. So an extra-sized jug, nearly full of old cider of the hardest and sourest kind, was put on the sled, and tied to one of the stakes, to keep it in place.

"Now, you children," said Mr. Hapley, as he was about starting, "you behave yourselves, all on you. You Sam, I want you to fodder them cows this noon, if I don't get home. And mother," he added, addressing his wife, "don't let Benny play out in the wet, he's got such a cold."

With these admonitions, the father departed. Unfortunately, there was no one to admonish him to behave himself, though perhaps he needed such a caution as much as his children. Arrived at the wood-lot, he and his assistant took a full "swig" from the jug, and then commenced work. By the time Mr. Hapley had felled one tree, he felt the need of another draught of cider; and seating himself on the prostrate trunk, he again tipped the jug, and then lighting his pipe, resigned himself to quiet contemplation. The sturdy strokes of his more industrious companion, if they reproached him, did not arouse him from his lazy lethargy for half an hour, and then he returned to his work only for a short time, soon seeking refreshment again from the jug and pipe. It was past noon when the sled was loaded up with green wood, and by this time, Mr. Hapley was in no amiable mood, the soothing influence of the pipe not having been equal to the exciting effects of the cider, which always made him as sour as itself. His companion, too, was not quite so cheery as when he came into the woods. He thought it rather hard fare, to do more than three-fourths of the work, and drink less than one-fourth of the cider. So they mounted the load, and drove home, scarcely speaking to each other on the way.

"My patience!" exclaimed Mrs. Hapley, as the team entered the yard; "have you brought me a load of green stuff, at this time of year, and not a stick of dry wood about the premises? What *shall* I do!"

"Do? why, you can stick it up in the chimney corner, and dry it," replied Mr. Hapley, quite unconcerned.

"Well," added his wife, with a sigh, "if I had only known you had no wood seasoning up in the lot, I'd have gone and cut some myself, sooner than try to burn that stuff."

"You're always a telling what *you'd* do," replied Mr. Hapley; "now I wish you'd go and do it, just once, and say nothin' about it. Plague on 't! how is a feller going to chop wood, when he's got the rheumatis' so he can't stand up? It seems as though women hadn't no consideration about some things."

Mrs. Hapley always refrained from bandying words with her husband, when he was in an irritable mood, and she made no further reply. He took the horses from the team, (for, according to his slack system, it was time enough to unload the wood, when the sled was needed again,) and led them into the barn. In a few moments he returned, and inquired, in a stern tone:—

"Who fed them cows, this noon?"

"I did," replied Mrs. Hapley. "Sam wasn't here, at noon, and so I took care of them."

"Just the way with that plaguy Sam," added Mr. Hapley. "He's never about when anything's to be done. Here, Sam! Sam!" he called at the top of his voice; but Sam did not respond, and Mr. Hapley continued, "What did you give 'em such a mess of hay for? They've wasted more'n half of it, and got it all over the barn. I don't see what you was thinking of. We can't afford to litter the critters with hay, when it's as skerce as 'tis now."

"I don't think I gave them too much," replied Mrs. Hapley. "The fact is, they don't like the hay, and they wont eat it up clean."

"Where's Benny?" inquired Mr. Hapley, suddenly noticing that his youngest boy was absent.

"He's gone out to play," replied his wife.

"I told you not to let him go out in the slosh—he'll be sick ag'in, you see if he aint," said Mr. Hapley.

"He's dressed warmly, and got his thick boots on," replied Mrs. Hapley. "It is so pleasant that I thought it would do him good to be out a little while in the air."

Mr. Hapley withdrew to the barn, and was feeding his horses, when a loud scream from Benny startled him. Running to a window in the back of the barn, he saw the cause of the outcry. Sam had thrown Benny down in the snow, and was pushing him about in it, and rubbing it into his face and neck. They were by the roadside, a few rods from the barn. Mr. Hapley flew to the door, and called to Sam, but Benny's outcry drowned his voice. He then ran towards them, but Sam had finished the assault, concluding with a few vigorous kicks, before he saw his father approaching. Mr. Hapley was so enraged at what he had witnessed, that he could hardly listen to a word of explanation. Benjamin, a lad of nine years, was his youngest child, and was supposed by the rest of the family to be the father's favorite. He was not at this time in robust health, which added to Mr. Hapley's excitement, on seeing him abused by Sam. The origin of the assault, which Mr. H. did not stop to investigate fully, was this. Benny, seeing his brother coming up the road, hid himself behind a stone wall, until he had passed, and then playfully threw a soft snow-ball at him, which chanced to hit him on the head, though not with much force. Sam instantly started for his little brother, who fled; but overtaking him, the unfeeling boy pitched him into a snow bank, and rolled him in it, then "washed his face in snow," sprinkled several handfuls of the fleecy element down his neck and back, and finally kicked him, as has been stated.

Mr. Hapley led the boys as far as the barn, and after telling Benny to go into the house, and ask his mother to take care of him, he pushed Sam into the barn, assuring him that *he* would attend to him. Having closed the doors, he ordered Sam to take off his coat, but the refractory boy refused. Enraged at this, the father seized him, and a desperate struggle ensued, the boy resisting even to blows, and the anger of the other waxing fiercer every moment. But Mr. Hapley was a powerful man, and the result of the contest was not long in doubt. The coat was stripped from the boy's back, and despite his efforts to escape, he soon found himself bound hand and foot to a post, utterly helpless. As it was useless to struggle, he now betook himself to yelling, which he did with such effect that all the family were soon drawn to the spot. But Mr. Hapley sternly ordered them all away, and then taking a heavy cart whip, commenced beating the boy with great severity. Soon the cries of the sufferer again brought the mother and the younger children to the spot, and despite the father's commands, Mrs. Hapley and Jessie entered the barn, and with tears pleaded for Sam. But the father, whose natural feelings were now blunted and benumbed by liquor, and whose wrath was stirred almost to its lowest depths by the resistance Sam had offered, took no notice of the sympathizing intruders, but kept on with the cruel punishment.

Marcus, who had heard the first outcry, and suspected the nature of the trouble, ran at once over to Mr. Hapley's, and entered the barn just at this juncture. The mother and daughter both besought him to interpose in behalf of the unfortunate boy, whose shirt was already slightly stained with blood. On his entrance, however, Mr. Hapley stayed his hand, and, looking somewhat abashed, as Marcus thought, inquired—

"What do you want here, sir?"

"Don't you think you have punished Sam about enough?" inquired Marcus, mildly.

"I guess I can flog my children without any advice from you—you'd better go home and mind your business," was the reply.

"I didn't mean any offence, Mr. Hapley," continued Marcus, in the same calm tone. "I heard Sam screaming, and I thought I would run over and see what the matter was, for I didn't know but somebody was abusing him. You would have done the same thing, if you had been in my place, Mr. Hapley."

"I wouldn't punish him any more, now, father," said Mrs. Hapley; "I think it's time to stop when the blood runs."

"Are you sorry for what you did?" inquired the father, addressing Sam.

"Yes," replied the boy, in a surly tone.

"Well, then, I'll let you off, with this," said Mr. Hapley. "But mind you, you wont get off so easy another time, if you don't behave yourself, so look out. I've let you alone till you're almost sp'ilt, but I'm going to turn over a new leaf with you, now. You've got to toe the mark, or else I'll put the marks onto your back—one of the two."

Mr. Hapley, as he said this, unbound the boy, who, on being released, went into the house, followed by his mother and the children. Marcus, finding himself alone with the misguided father, thought it his duty to address a word of remonstrance to him against such punishments.

"Mr. Hapley," he said, "do you think this is the best way to discipline a boy? Isn't it a rather harsh remedy?"

"I wont have nothing to say to you or anybody else about that," responded Mr. Hapley. "It's nobody's business if I choose to whip my boy, and I wish folks would mind their own affairs, and let me alone. I guess I'm old enough to know what I'm about, and if I aint, I don't want your advice."

"I am aware no one has a right to interfere," replied Marcus, "unless you *abuse* your child. In that case I suppose you know the law will protect him. If you didn't abuse Sam, just now, I think you came very near it."

"What's that?" exclaimed Mr. Hapley. "Do you come over here to sarce me, in my own premises, you young upstart?"

"I see it is of no use to talk with you now, Mr. Hapley," Marcus calmly replied, and then withdrew.

The next morning, Jessie, with tears in her eyes, informed Marcus that her brother was missing. He had evidently gone off in the night, intending to seek his fortune elsewhere, for he had taken a change of clothing. Before starting for the academy, Marcus called on the Hapleys to see if he could be of any service to them, in their new trouble.

"No," said Mr. Hapley, gruffly, "we aint a going to send after that boy, nor no such thing. If he's a mind to run away, let him run, that's all. I'll warrant he'll get enough of it, and be glad to get home ag'in, before a month's out."

Mrs. Hapley looked anxious, and the children sad, though the father seemed quite unconcerned. No steps were taken to bring back the fugitive, or even to ascertain in what direction he had gone, and nothing was heard from him, until about a week after, when he suddenly made his appearance one evening. He was in a sorry plight, his feet being somewhat frosted, his clothes having suffered from rough usage, and he being very tired and hungry. His parents received him with unexpected kindness, and even Mr. Hapley himself was more pleased at his return than he was willing to confess. Sam, however, did not seem inclined to say much about his adventures, during his week's absence, and the curiosity of the family, on that point, was far from satisfied.

Two or three days after Sam's return, a couple of strangers drove up to the door, and having found Sam, told him he was their prisoner, at the same time showing him a writ authorizing his arrest. They also informed Mr. Hapley that they were empowered to search the house for stolen property; adding that a robbery had been committed in a town about ten miles distant, and there was reason to suspect his son had some connection with it. The shock of this intelligence so affected Mrs. Hapley, that she fainted. While her husband was using means for her recovery, the officers put a pair of hand-cuffs upon Sam's wrists, to prevent his escape, and then took him up into his chamber, where they commenced the search. There was an old bureau in the room, which they examined very thoroughly. They also scrutinized the boy's clothing, peered into the fire-place and up the chimney, looked for loose boards in the flooring, and examined holes in the plastering, but all to no purpose. They then overhauled the bed, and soon drew out from among the feathers a package which was found to contain a breast-pin, several silver spoons, and a watch. With this they announced themselves as satisfied, and soon started off with their prisoner.

The news of Sam's arrest spread through the village like wild-fire. Marcus heard of it as soon as he was out of school, in the afternoon. On the way home, he overtook Jessie and Kate, who, full of spirits, wondered that Marcus should be so sober. The sad news was not broken to Jessie until she entered her home, where she found her father upon the floor, drunk, and her mother sick in her bed, while Benny was silently weeping, as though his heart were breaking. Henry alone was able to explain to her what had happened. The poor girl could hardly help sinking to the floor, as Henry related his story; but feeling that this was no time to give way to her emotions, she controlled her nerves with admirable coolness, and soon partly forgot her own sorrow, in her efforts to relieve the others. She prepared some medicine for her mother; put a pillow under her father's head, having tried in vain to assist him to a chair; spread an old coat over him, to prevent his taking cold; spoke a few words of comfort to Benny; and then proceeded to get supper.

It was soon whispered about town that Mr. Hapley, since the arrest of his son, had abandoned himself to his cups worse than ever. Several of his neighbors kindly remonstrated with him against the course he was pursuing, and urged him to take some steps in aid of his misguided boy; but their efforts were all in vain. Although Sam's trial was to come on in a few days, none of his friends had been near him, to offer him advice or assistance. In this extremity, Mrs. Hapley appealed to Marcus for assistance, who readily consented to do all he could in behalf of the boy. The next day he drove over to the town where Sam was awaiting his trial, accompanied by Mrs. Hapley. They found the boy alone in a cell, looking very dejected. He burst into tears, on seeing his mother, and for several minutes neither of them could speak. Marcus, in a kind tone, told him they had come to see if they could do anything for him, and urged him to tell them frankly all about the stolen property found in his room, that they might the better know how to proceed. Sam at once expressed his willingness to do so, and then related his adventures, from the time he left home until his return. His story, in substance, was as follows.

He left home on a pleasant moonlight night, as soon as he was satisfied all the family were asleep. He walked seven or eight miles, and then forced an entrance into a barn, where he slept the rest of the night. The family gave him a breakfast, the next morning, and he then resumed his journey. In the course of the forenoon he reached a large town, where he concluded to stop and see what he could do; for he had but half a dollar in his pocket, and began to feel a little uneasy. There was a large tavern in the village, which was much frequented by sleighing parties, and for a day or two Sam managed to pick up a little change, by holding horses, and performing other small chores for the company. He was allowed to sleep in the barn, and got his meals at a low "saloon" near by. The associates among whom he was thus thrown, were not of the best kind, and one of them, a young man several years older than himself, was an offender against the law, having served out two or three sentences in jails. His name was Mack. There was something in the face, the conversation, or the peculiar circumstances of Sam, that led him to propose to the boy a sort of partnership in crime; and as he set forth the gains to be derived from such a course in the brightest colors, the boy's easy virtue made but slight resistance, and without much persuasion, he agreed to the proposition.

The next night after the matter had been settled, Sam made his first attempt as a burglar, in connection with Mack. They chose for the scene of operations a large and substantial house, occupied by a widow of reputed wealth, and her family of young children. The moon shone bright, but as the house was in a retired neighborhood, they thought they could elude detection. Mack entered the dwelling first, by a second story window, standing upon Sam's broad shoulders to reach the sash, which proved not to be fastened down. He then descended to the basement, and opened the doors, that they might easily escape in case of alarm. Sam now entered, and the two ransacked the lower part of the house, helping themselves to a quantity of silver ware, some jewelry, two watches, and a good supper. After securing a few articles of value, Sam was in haste to escape, but his companion seemed in no hurry, and went about the house as leisurely as though he were at home. This free and easy bearing doubtless seemed quite professional to Mack, but he happened to carry it a little too far for his own safety. Sam, impatient of his dilatory movements, was awaiting him outside, when he heard a movement in the house which led him to take flight. It seemed the widow had been awakened by the burglars, and, arousing her oldest son, a brave boy of fourteen, they descended as noiselessly as possible. Mack had just before lighted a lamp, and gone down into the cellar, to see if he could find a bottle of wine, leaving his plunder on the kitchen table. Suddenly the cellar door was closed and locked upon him, and he heard strange voices, one of which, the voice of a boy, assured him that he had a loaded rifle, and would put a bullet through him "in less than no time," if he attempted to get away. The burglar tried to escape by a window, but the rifle was quickly pointed at him, outside, and he gave up the attempt. In a few moments help arrived, and he was secured. As all the stolen property was not found, it was suspected that he had an accomplice, though he refused to give any information on that point.

Sam left the village as speedily as possible, directing his steps towards a town where he had never been before. After wandering about two days, and suffering much from fatigue, cold, hunger, and anxiety, he at length reached home, as we have seen. The sudden and unexplained disappearance of Sam, from the village tavern, together with the fact that he had been seen with Mack several times on the evening of the burglary, directed suspicion towards him, and finally led to his arrest.

After hearing Sam's story, Marcus expressed the opinion that he had better plead guilty, and frankly own up his offence to the officers of justice. This advice was accepted by Sam and his mother. Marcus and Mrs. Hapley then secured a lawyer to appear on behalf of the boy at the trial; and they also had an interview with the officer who conducted the prosecution, explaining to him the circumstances of the case, and soliciting his influence in favor of the prisoner, on the ground that this was his first offence, and that he had been led astray by a hardened offender.

Sam was brought before the court a day or two after, and pleaded guilty to the charge of burglary. His counsel urged several reasons for a light sentence, and the prosecuting attorney said that, under the circumstances, he should not oppose the request. The judge, however, thought it was not exactly a case for mercy. The prisoner, he said, was a runaway from home. He had voluntarily made himself a vagrant, and had shown his willingness to resort to crime, to get a living. No attempt had been made to prove a good character for him, and he doubted whether such an attempt could succeed. He concluded by sentencing the boy to the county jail for four months.

CHAPTER XVI.

MERRY DAYS AND SAD ONES.

"I DON'T care, I got the start of all of you," said Ronald, as the family were discussing over the breakfast table, Christmas morning, the question who was the first to wish the others "a merry Christmas." "I heard the clock strike four, and I jumped right out of bed, and ran into the entry, and wished you all a merry Christmas."

"Well, that wasn't fair—I was asleep, and didn't hear you," said Kate.

"So was I asleep," "And I," "And I," added one and another.

"That makes no difference, so long as *I* was awake," replied Ronald.

"Ronald," said Marcus, "reminds me of a fellow I have either heard or dreamed about, who bragged that he got up and wished all the kingdoms of the earth a happy new year at one lick. For my part, if any body has got any good wishes for me, I should prefer to be informed of it when I am awake. And I don't care much about being lumped in with all the kingdoms of the earth, either."

"Well, sir, I wish you a merry Christmas, *all to yourself,*—I believe you are awake now," said Ronald, with a sly chuckle.

"There, I may as well give in—I wont try to say anything more," added Marcus, as the laugh went round the table at his expense.

After breakfast no little curiosity was excited by a package which Marcus handed to Oscar. It was received by Marcus the day before, by express, with a note requesting him to deliver it to Oscar, Christmas morning. After removing sundry cords and wrappers, the contents stood disclosed. There was a fine pair of skates, from his father; a gold pen, from his mother; a pair of wrought slippers, from Alice, his oldest sister; a beautiful book-mark from Ella, another sister; a book from his brother Ralph; and a package of confectionery from George, his youngest brother. Brief notes accompanied several of the presents. There were also two letters in the package, the handwriting of one of which, Oscar did not recognize. It proved to be from a young acquaintance in Boston named William Davenport, who went by the familiar name of "Whistler" among his comrades. It was written in fulfilment of a promise he had made, before Oscar left Boston. The other letter was from his mother, and, like all similar favors from that source, was full, margin and all, of kind words, good advice, and family news. It contained an item of intelligence, however, that cast something of a damper over the spirits of Oscar. It was as follows:—

"The brig Susan has been heard from at last. You know we have been looking for her ever since October. She foundered in a gale in September, off the South American coast, and the men took to the boats. One of the boats was picked up, after floating about for several days, and the men in it were saved, after enduring great hardships, and have arrived here. Nothing has been heard of the other boat, on board which was poor Jerry. His parents are much distressed about him; but your father thinks he may be safe yet, as the boat may have reached the shore, or may have fallen in with some outward-bound vessel. Let us hope for the best, as long as we can."

The "poor Jerry" referred to, was a cousin to Oscar. The two boys had once been very intimate, somewhat to the damage of Jerry's character; and it was in a great measure owing to this intimacy that Jerry absconded from his home, in Brookdale, about a year previous to this time, and shipped for a voyage around Cape Horn.

There was to be a children's Christmas party at the town hall, in the evening, and the presents designed for the other members of the family were reserved to grace the "tree" that was to be one of the chief attractions of the occasion. Marcus and the children constituted a part of the committee of arrangements for the festival, and were occupied with their duties through a good part of the day. At an early hour in the evening, the whole family proceeded to the town hall, where they found the chief portion of the town's population assembled, especially the younger part. The hall, with its evergreen decorations, its numerous lights, and its sea of happy faces, presented an enlivening spectacle. At the hour appointed for opening the exercises, the clergyman of the village ascended the platform, and after a few remarks, invoked a blessing upon those assembled. Then came an introductory declamation, by one of the academy boys, followed by the recitation of an appropriate poem by a fair-haired little girl of six summers. Next appeared upon the platform our two young friends Ronald and Otis, who confronted each other in blank silence a minute or two, and then retreated to the ante-room, without exchanging a word. Some of the audience were in painful suspense, during this scene, supposing it to be a failure; while others began to whisper that it was a tableau, and not a dialogue, though they were puzzled to tell what it represented, or why the figures should walk to and from the stage, in sight of the audience.

A curtain before the platform now fell, and after a few minutes was again raised, disclosing to the audience a charming tableau of Minnehaha, the Indian maid. The two boys who had acted in the mute scene, just before, now re-appeared, and went through very creditably with a dialogue, Ronald, the leading speaker, having suddenly forgotten his part, on his first appearance. Then followed several songs, declamations and tableaux, after which the main attraction of the evening was introduced, by the raising of the curtain which concealed the Christmas tree from view. A loud and merry shout arose from the young folks, which was prolonged for a minute or two, and followed by general expressions of admiration from all present. There stood the tree, a tall, straight and symmetrical evergreen, illuminated with candles, arrayed among its branches, and adorned with artificial icicles and snow flakes. The fruits, however, with which every bough and twig seemed bending, were the most interesting objects of contemplation to the hundred pairs of youthful eyes fixed earnestly upon the tree. Many of these fruits, it is true, were hidden from sight, by a rind of paper, cloth or wood; but imagination readily supplied all deficiencies of this kind, and the little eyes gazed, and sparkled, and longed, just as though they pierced through all the outer coverings that concealed the tempting clusters which hung upon the boughs.

After a few moments, Santa Claus suddenly appeared, and walking across the platform, took his station by the side of the tree, amid rapturous applause from the company. He appeared to be a venerable personage, with a flowing gray beard, and was completely encased in furs, from top to toe— fur boots, fur leggings, fur tunic, fur mittens, and a fur cap which enveloped all of his head except the face. After silence had been secured, he spoke, in tones which seemed very soft and gentle to proceed from so rough and ancient a personage, and which not a few of the audience declared "sounded just like the voice of Marcus Page." He said he had brought "heaps" of presents, and had almost broken his back with the effort. He hoped he had brought something for everybody; but if he had not, he trusted they would not blame him, for he had done the best he could. He requested the children not to crowd around the tree, and invited the recipients to walk up one by one as their names were called. He then commenced gathering the fruit, to each of which was attached the name of the person it was intended for. And now the sport began in earnest. What a queer assortment of articles to gather from one tree! There were gold rings, breastpins, lockets, pencils, and pens; silver spoons and thimbles; work-boxes, wooden dogs, and stuffed rabbits; books, fancy boxes, and popped corn; sleds, skates, and mittens; pin-cushions, needle-books, and bags of candy; dolls, pocket knives and cologne bottles. But time and patience would fail to mention half the things that good Santa Claus handed down to the company. It was an hour before the distribution was finished. The company then adjourned to the room below, where they found an abundance of simple country refreshments provided. A speech or two followed, and with three cheers for Christmas day, and three more for Santa Claus, the entertainment ended.

There was the usual exchange of good wishes and little keep-sakes, on New Year's morning, but the day was not otherwise distinguished as a festival, and the schools kept, and business went on, as on other days. As the family were seated at the breakfast table, a light rap upon the door was heard, and on answering the call, Jessie Hapley, pale and agitated, was found upon the steps.

"Mrs. Page," she said, as soon as that lady appeared, "mother wants to know if you will come right over—she is afraid Benny is dying;" and the poor girl burst into tears as she delivered the message.

"Benny dying!" exclaimed Mrs. Page, "why, I had no idea he was so sick as that—how long has he been so?"

"He grew worse very fast last night," replied Jessie. "Henry has gone for the doctor, and mother thought perhaps you could tell what to do, till he comes."

"Yes, I will go over immediately," replied Mrs. Page, and she went for her bonnet and shawl, and a minute after started by the shortest cut across the fields for the house of sorrow.

Marcus would gladly have accompanied his mother, but for fear that his presence at such a time might be regarded an intrusion. Benny was one of a class of little boys which Marcus had instructed in the Sabbath school for some two years. Partly from the gentle, winning disposition of the child, and partly on account of the unfavorable influences to which he was exposed at home, Marcus felt an especial interest in him, and had watched his decline with no little solicitude. For several months past, Benny had been able to attend the Sabbath school only occasionally; but every Sunday his young teacher carried or sent to him an attractive book from the library, and in other ways manifested his continued interest in the sick scholar. It was with a heavy heart, therefore, that Marcus heard his mother summoned to Benny's death-bed, on this pleasant New Year's morning. An hour later, on his way to the academy, he stopped at Mr. Hapley's door, to inquire after the patient, and was told that the doctor was still with him, and that the result of his efforts in behalf of the boy was yet uncertain.

In spite of the pleasant associations of the day, and the kindly greetings with which his scholars met him, a cloud hung over the spirits of Marcus, which he was unable to dispel. One incident occurred, however, which was peculiarly grateful to his feelings. On entering the school-room, he was followed by Harrison Clark, who, taking from behind a blackboard a handsomely finished cane, handed it to Marcus, and, with some embarrassment in his manner, said:—

"Mr. Page, will you accept of this as a New Year's present? It isn't of much value, but I made it myself on purpose for you."

"Ah, is this your work?" inquired Marcus, carefully examining the article, which was really well made, in every part. "Did you do it all yourself—head, ferule, rings and all?"

"Yes, sir—Mr. Tucker let me use his tools, and I did the whole of the work myself," replied Harrison.

"It is certainly very creditable to you," continued Marcus. "I don't see how it could be improved. Yes, I will accept it with great pleasure, and thank you for it, too. Coming as a present from you, I shall value it ten times what it would cost to get such a cane made—yes, a hundred times. I shall remember your kindness with gratitude, perhaps after you have forgotten both me and the cane."

"I don't think I shall forget you very soon—you have been so good to me," replied the boy, with a look which testified to the sincerity of the remark.

"And you have proved yourself worthy of my kindness, so I need not take much credit for that," rejoined Marcus.

The boy, who but lately was so bold and defiant in his bearing, blushed at this not unmeaning compliment, and withdrew.

When Marcus returned home, in the afternoon, he again stopped to inquire after the sick boy, and was requested to go in, as Benny had expressed a desire to see him. He found the sufferer in a little bed which had been made up for him in the front room, near the fire, for he complained much of the cold. A faint smile lit up his face as Marcus entered.

"How is he, Mrs. Hapley?" inquired Marcus, as he seated himself by the bedside, and took Benny's cold hand into his own.

"I think he is a little more comfortable than he was this morning," replied Mrs. Hapley. "He has been very much distressed for breath, most of the day, but he seems to be better, now."

"I am glad to hear that, and I hope he will continue to improve," said Marcus.

Benny, whose mild, lustrous eyes had been fastened upon Marcus from the moment he entered the door, was too weak to speak aloud; but as he seemed to have something to say, Marcus bent his ear down to the boy's mouth, and was addressed in a whisper as follows:—

"I'm not going to get well, and I don't want to. I'm going to heaven pretty soon. I have been longing to go, ever since I was taken sick, and now I know I'm almost there. I love God, and Jesus, and the angels, and all good folks. Do you remember what you told me about heaven, the other day—how many millions of good little children are there, and how Jesus calls them his lambs, and wipes away their tears, and takes them in his arms? There wont he anything to make us sorry in heaven, will there?"

"No," replied Marcus, his mind recurring to that passage of Scripture, "There shall be no more death, neither sorrow, nor crying, neither shall there be any more pain."

There was a brief interval of silence, broken only by an occasional half-suppressed sigh that escaped from Jessie, who was seated in a remote corner of the room, and by the slow and regular tread of Mr. Hapley, who was pacing the floor of the chamber overhead, in an agony of grief and remorse. Marcus afterwards learned that a few hours before this, when Benny was thought to be dying, he had entreated his father in a most affectionate and touching manner to abandon the besetting sin which was bringing himself and his family to ruin and disgrace. The strong man, after a brief but desperate struggle, promised the dying boy that he would abandon his cups from that hour, and would try to live in such a way that he might meet his little son in heaven.

Mrs. Hapley, who had been engaged in the kitchen, now came in, with a bottle of hot water, to be applied to Benny's feet; but he whispered to her:—

"O, mother, I am *so* cold! Wont you take me up in your arms, and hold me before the fire?"

"Yes, dear," replied his mother, and she took the boy gently into her arms, wrapped a blanket around him, and sat down before the blazing fire.

This movement seemed to be too much for the boy, for he gasped for breath, and sank exhausted into his mother's arms. After a few minutes he recovered sufficiently to speak.

"Why, mother," he said, "how fast it grows dark! I can't hardly see anything."

"Jessie, ask your father to come down," said Mrs. Hapley, trying to speak calmly.

"It is dark here, but it is light *there*—O, how light!" whispered the dying boy.

"Where?" inquired the mother, scarcely knowing what she asked.

"I don't know where it is," replied the boy. "I saw it coming, way off, just now, like a bright cloud, and now it's all around me. Why, mother, don't you see it? The room is all full of it!"

Mr. Hapley now entered the room, but, seemingly unable to endure the scene, silently bowed his head against the wall. Jessie and Henry also came in with their father.

"I want to kiss you all," whispered Benny to his mother, after the family had assembled.

His wish was complied with, and his mother, father, Jessie, Henry and Marcus successively received and returned a parting kiss.

"Now one more for Sammy—you'll give it to him when he comes back, wont you, mother?" added Benny.

The promise was made, and the kiss given. But the poor boy did not know that his absent brother was at that moment serving a sentence in jail as a convicted felon. The result of Sam's trial had been wisely concealed from Benny, on account of his illness.

The circle had sat in silence for several minutes, when Mrs. Hapley arose, and tenderly laying her precious charge upon the bed, kissed the pale brow, and said, in a low, calm tone, which almost startled herself:—

"It is all over—the bitterness of death is past!"

The spirit of the child had departed so peacefully, that she could not tell when he drew the last breath. But the true and loving heart had ceased to beat, and the mild eyes were set in death, and the last enemy had accomplished his work surely, though noiselessly.

Marcus soon withdrew from the sorrowing circle, his own heart bowed in grief as sincere if not as deep as that of the near relatives of the deceased. It was the first time he had ever come into the immediate presence of death, and had seen, as it were, the fatal arrow wing its way into the living mark. It was, indeed, the first time that the grave had claimed one in whom he felt so deep an interest, and towards whom he held so near a relation; for he never could realize the death of his father, followed as it was by years of anxious suspense and hope deferred, and shrouded in impenetrable mystery up to this hour.

Mrs. Page and her sister went over to comfort and assist the stricken family, while Marcus retired to his chamber, to commune with his own thoughts. Though far from unfaithful to his trust as a religious teacher, he now lamented that he had done so little for the spiritual improvement of the dear boy whom death had just removed from the reach of his influence. Never before did he realize so vividly the uncertainty of life, the insignificance of worldly ambition, and the inestimable value of those treasures which make us "rich toward God." And now, at the beginning of the new year, did he kneel down and ask for divine aid, as he pledged himself to strive, with more fidelity than ever before, to kindle in the young minds around him desires after a higher and purer life.

CHAPTER XVII.

ADVERSITY.

THE first act of Mr. Hapley, after Benny was laid in the frozen ground, was one that gave new hope to the sorrowing household. At his request, the clergyman of the village had previously written a pledge of total abstinence from all intoxicating liquor, which the afflicted father signed upon the coffin of his boy. On returning from the funeral, he collected together all the alcoholic liquors in the house, consisting of cider, whiskey and brandy, and taking them into the yard, poured them out upon the snow. As Mrs. Hapley and the children gazed upon this novel scene, they almost forgot their bereavement, in the new hopes and joys which seemed now about to be bestowed upon them. And well might they take courage. Mr. Hapley had thus far sacredly kept his promise to Benny. He was very sad, and his limbs were weak and trembling, and there was a terrible craving and gnawing within, that neither food nor ordinary drink could satisfy; still he struggled manfully against the tempter, and friends not a few stood by, with words of encouragement and cheer. Indeed, with his sober and subdued air, his clean-shaven face, and the general tidiness of his personal appearance, he already seemed like a different man.

The reformation of Mr. Hapley was much talked of among his neighbors and acquaintances, and very different opinions were expressed as to its permanence. It was generally thought that he would persevere, but there were some who had little faith in his good purposes. Old Mr. Todd, who held a mortgage on his farm, and who was regarded as quite an oracle, shook his head in a knowing manner, when the matter was mentioned at the post office, one morning.

"I've known Charles Hapley," said he, "ever since he was a boy, and I knew his father before him. The old man had the best farm in town, but the family has been gradually running down these twenty years, and it's my opinion that Hapley will die a drunkard, as his father did."

"Now, Squire," said an elderly and benevolent looking man, who was seated on the counter, "it appears to me you are a little too hard on Hapley. They say he's stuck it out for more'n a week, and not touched a drop of anything, and that's doing pretty well, for him. I hold that we all ought to encourage the poor fellow along, and not go around predicting that he'll die a drunkard."

"So do I hold to encouraging him along," replied Mr. Todd; "but at the same time I don't believe it will do any good. He never did have any control over himself, from a boy, and I don't believe he's going to keep the bridle on a great while, now. You see if he does, that's all."

"Guess the old man means to step in there," said some one, as Mr. Todd went his way.

"Yes, it's plain enough what he's after," said another.

The speakers alluded to Mr. Todd's taking possession of the Hapley farm, on account of the non-payment of his mortgage. Their conclusion was not a very charitable one, to be sure. Nor was it exactly kind in Mr. Todd to predict with so much assurance the relapse of Mr. Hapley. Still, it must be admitted that he had pretty strong ground for his opinion, though he need not have been so free to express it. The lesson of self-government is a hard one to learn in mature life, especially to a man who has for many years been tyrannized over by depraved appetites and passions. The position of such a man is something like that of Mazeppa, the young page of a Polish king, who for some offence was lashed, naked, to the back of a wild horse, which was then set free, and plunged with frightful speed through forest and plain into his native country, bearing his helpless and well-nigh lifeless rider with him. But when the appetites and passions are the ruled, and not the rulers, they may be compared to the same steed, tamed and docile, bridled and saddled, and ready to do your bidding. Mazeppa, it is true, had the good fortune to survive the painful ordeal, and lived to become a prince; but we think few would be willing to run such a race, even for such a prize, except upon the wild horses of their own ungovernable passions.

But Mr. Todd proved a true prophet, in this instance. In less than a fortnight after Benny's death, Mr. Hapley came home from the village one afternoon sadly intoxicated. How he happened to fall, was never explained to the family. He had been to the store where liquors were sold, on business, and probably the wretched sensation in his stomach, aided by the sight and smell of the tempter, the associations of the place, and perhaps the coaxings of the drunkard-maker, suddenly swept away the breastwork of good purposes he had erected. He tasted—he fell; and what a death-blow was that act to the hopes and peace of his poor wife and children! To Mrs. Hapley and Jessie, especially, it seemed as if the last hope had been swept away.

The next day, when Mr. Hapley realized his situation, he was overcome with grief and shame. He was, moreover, discouraged. He had lost both his self-respect and his self-reliance. He had no longer any confidence in his ability to keep the pledge. Meanwhile his thirst for the deadly liquid was growing more insupportable for the fresh stimulus it had received. In this pitiable state of mind and body, he went again in the afternoon to the rum-shop, and attempted to drown his sorrow in a still deeper potation. Towards night, a severe snow-storm set in, but he did not return. Hour after hour did his wife sit at the fire, after the children had retired, listening for his return; but the wild shriek of the wind, as the storm waxed more furious, and the sharp rattle of the snow against the window panes, were the only sounds she heard. At length, when it was almost midnight, unable longer to bear the terrible suspense, she aroused Henry from his sleep, and told him to go over to Mrs. Page's, and ask Marcus if he would not take a horse and go in search of the missing man. The boy dressed himself, and plunged into the huge snow-drifts. He had not proceeded far, however, before he began to doubt whether he should be able either to go on or to return. Blinded by the driving storm, transfixed by cutting blasts, the divisions between roads and fields quite obliterated, and floundering in snow up to his arm-pits, he sank exhausted, more than once, into the hole he had made; but with the energy of despair, he again aroused himself, and at length reached Mrs. Page's door-steps.

After considerable effort, some of the family were aroused, and Marcus, on learning Henry's errand, at once prepared to go out in search of his father. He concluded he could get along best on horseback; and putting a bridle on Charley, the toughest of the two horses, he mounted him, and taking Henry behind him, carried him home. He then set out for the village, by the route Mr. Hapley had probably taken, which led him directly into the teeth of the storm. But he found it impossible to keep in the road, and his horse soon began to sink into old drifts newly buried, and to flounder among invisible stones, stumps, fences and pitfalls, until, at last, the exhausted creature seemed unable to proceed further. Marcus was accordingly obliged to give up the search, of which fact he informed Mrs. Hapley, before returning home.

The storm moderated in the morning, but owing to the state of the roads, several hours elapsed before arrangements could be made to search for the missing man. In the course of the forenoon, he was found, about a quarter of a mile from the road, sitting in his sleigh, with the reins in his hands; but the rider and his horse were both frozen stiff. The horse had apparently been thrown down by a log, and was unable to rise without assistance, which the unfortunate rider was too insensible or too benumbed to render. So they perished there alone, and were well-nigh buried from sight before they were discovered. A jug of rum, found in the sleigh, furnished a sad clue to the catastrophe, had any been needed.

The next day, a new grave was opened in the frozen earth, by the side of Benny's, and the father was laid close by the son he had so lately promised to meet in heaven, and to whom he had pledged himself to a reformed life. O, how sad is *such* a funeral, when hope, and honor, and happiness, are consigned to the tomb with the remains of the lost! Truly, in such a case "'tis the survivor dies."

It is often said that misfortunes never come singly. So, indeed, did it prove in the case of this family. The property left by Mr. Hapley was barely sufficient to pay his debts; and as most of it was mortgaged, very little remained for the family. Notwithstanding these reverses, Jessie continued to attend the academy, and was still "trying to be somebody," as Abby Leonard contemptuously expressed it, though that young lady, it should be added, now manifested something like pity for the heart-stricken girl. And in spite of the drawbacks to which she had been subjected, Jessie maintained a high rank in her class, winning the respect alike of teachers and scholars, as she also did their sympathy and good-will. But there were few among her gay-hearted school-mates who could half realize the sorrows, and disappointments, and discouragements, that were mingled in her cup.

On returning from school one afternoon, she found traces of weeping on the face of her mother, which the latter for a time declined to explain. The reason, however, came out after a while. On the death of Mr. Hapley, as he left no will, an administrator was appointed, according to law, to settle up his estate; that is, to take charge of the property, ascertain and pay the debts, and deliver the balance, if any, to the lawful heirs. This administrator was a kind-hearted man named Allen, who had always shown himself very friendly to Mrs. Hapley. It seemed Mr. Allen had called upon her, that afternoon, to talk about her husband's affairs. There was, he said, but little more than sufficient property to pay off the mortgages. He advised her, therefore, to give up the farm, to sell all the personal property they could dispense with, and to find homes for herself and children elsewhere. The children, he said, were all old enough to support themselves, and she need have no one but herself to look out for.

"Well, mother, that's only what I expected," said Jessie, when the matter was explained; "we couldn't carry on the farm, if we should stay here, and we may as well go somewhere else. Grandpa said he would give you a home; Henry can get a chance to live with some farmer, and work for his board and clothes; Sam can earn his living, if he chooses to; and as for me, I will go to some factory town and work in a mill, and in a little time I shall be able to support you, as well as myself."

"And give up your hope of becoming a teacher?" inquired her mother.

"Perhaps not," replied Jessie. "I may be able to fit myself for teaching, even in a mill. Girls *have* done such things, and why not I?"

"But I never can let you go off alone into a factory," said Mrs. Hapley. "If you go, I must go, too."

"Well, mother," added Jessie, after a pause, "we'll manage to get along some how, only don't let us get discouraged. We know it is all for the best, and every thing will come out right in the end. When I feel sad, I repeat to myself that beautiful hymn Mr. Merrill read at Benny's funeral—do you remember it, mother?" and Jessie recited the following verses:—

"O Father, good or evil send,

As seemeth best to thee,

And teach my stubborn soul to bend

In love to thy decree.

"Whatever come, if thou wilt bless

The brightness and the gloom,

And temper joy, and soothe distress,

I fear no earthly doom.

"Life cannot give a cureless sting,

Death can but crown my bliss,

And waft me far, on angel's wing,

To perfect happiness."

Jessie's uncomplaining spirit, her readiness to sacrifice her most cherished hopes, and her beautiful, child-like faith in God, shed a sweet and soothing influence upon the fainting and murmuring heart of the mother. A little while after, Henry came in from school, and for a moment looked rather sad, when he was told that the family had got to remove and be broken up, very soon; but he quickly recovered his good spirits, saying:—

"Well, mother, I don't care much, after all. Let Mr. Todd have the old farm if he wants it—it's all run out, and we couldn't do anything if we staid here. I know I can earn my living, if anybody will give me a chance, and one of these days I'll have a good deal better farm than this—you see if I don't! Then you and Jessie shall come and live with me, and we'll all be together again."

Henry soon found a chance to earn his living, for Mr. Allen agreed to take him into his family at once, and maintain him in return for his services. As to Jessie, everybody said it was too bad to send her off to a mill, and after some little consultation, Mrs. Page proposed a plan by which this might be avoided. Ellen Blake, who had lived with the Page family for some time, was about to return home, on account of the sickness of her mother. It was proposed to let Jessie occupy her place in the family, working for her board, until she should finish preparing herself for a teacher. She was to attend the academy two or three terms more, and when not engaged in her studies, was to render all the assistance to Mrs. Page she could. Her mother was to clothe her, during this period, and it was thought that after the present term she could render some assistance in the lower department, and thus secure her own tuition free. When this plan was proposed to Jessie, she seemed very grateful for the kindness which prompted so liberal an offer, but was unwilling to accept of it, fearing she could make no adequate return for her board. It was only after considerable persuasion that she consented to the arrangement. When the matter was finally settled, Mrs. Hapley concluded to accept an invitation to go to her father's, in a neighboring town, and make that her home until she could do something for her own support.

CHAPTER XVIII.

THE DIALOGUE.

THE winter term of the academy was now drawing towards an end, and preparations were already commenced for the closing examination and exhibition. Thus far the term had been a very harmonious and prosperous one, and the students, with but few exceptions, had made good progress. There seemed, indeed, to be an unusual ambition and rivalry in some of the classes. One morning, the following line from Dr. Young was found, written in a large hand on the most conspicuous blackboard in the room:—

"PRAISE NO MAN E'ER DESERVED, WHO SOUGHT NO MORE."

After the usual opening exercises, Mr. Upton called attention to it, saying it contained a truth which every scholar would do well to ponder. "If we aim at excellence as students," he added, "merely to secure praise, and to gain a prize, or for the love of excelling, we are giving ourselves up to a very mean and unworthy motive. Whatever we may accomplish or win, under the influence of such a base impulse, we shall really deserve neither praise nor reward. Can any of you explain what is the true and proper motive for the student?"

There was a pause. Finding no one was likely to respond, Jessie Hapley arose, and said:—

"I suppose we ought to seek knowledge because it is good, in itself, and because it will increase our usefulness, hereafter."

"That is a very good answer," replied Mr. Upton. "There may be other lawful motives for studying hard, such as a wish to please our parents and friends, or to better our condition in the world, or to gratify our own tastes; but the noblest and purest motive is that which Miss Hapley has given— knowledge is a good thing in itself, and is a mighty power for good, in the hands of one who aims to serve God and bless the world. Compared with such a motive as this, how contemptible is the ambition which seeks only to shine on examination day, or to outdo a rival, or take the highest prize! That we may bear this in mind, we will let this motto remain before us until the blackboard is needed for other purposes."

Ronald was a very good declaimer, as were several others of the boys in his class. Marcus had given him some encouragement that he would prepare an original dialogue for Ronald and a few of his classmates to bring out at the exhibition. This half-promise he was now reminded of, almost daily, until at length he agreed that if Ronald would find a suitable plot or subject for a dialogue, he would assist him in putting it upon paper. This, he said, was all he could promise to do, at present. Ronald was at first a little discouraged by this proposal; but setting his wits to work, in a day or two he suggested to Marcus a plan of a dialogue.

"I should think we might make something out of that," said Marcus, after Ronald had explained the plan. "Now you sit down, and write out a rough outline of it, and then let me see it."

"But you said you would help me write it out," said Ronald.

"So I will," replied Marcus; "but I want you to do what you can, first, without my help. After you have made your first draft, we will go over it together, and see what improvements we can make in it."

"But I can't do it—I don't know where to begin," pleaded Ronald.

"O, yes, you can," replied Marcus. "Write it out just as you explained it to me, and that will he a good beginning."

Ronald at length mustered courage enough to make the attempt. His dialogue was of course quite imperfect, but it served as a good basis for Marcus to work upon. Two or three evenings were spent over it, by the joint authors, before it was pronounced satisfactory. When completed, the ideas and incidents of the piece were for the most part Ronald's, while they were indebted to Marcus for much of the language in which they were clothed, and for the general arrangement they assumed.

The following is a copy of the dialogue, as it read when completed. The part which Ronald decided to take was that of "*Joseph Foot*," as his powers of mimicry enabled him to imitate the backwoods dialect very successfully:

HEAD AND FOOT.

SCENE—*A school-room, with a class of ten or twelve boys, seated on a bench.* PRINCIPAL CHARACTERS—JOHN HEAD, *who is at the head of the class, and* JOSEPH FOOT, *a wonderfully good-natured backwoods lad, who is at the other extremity.*

HEAD [*rising, and holding in his hand something concealed in a cloth.*]—Friends and classmates! We have passed through the dread ordeal of another examination. Our grave and reverend seigniors have set in solemn inquisition over us, to their hearts' content. They have weighed us, and gauged us, and tested us, and dissected and analyzed us, till we feel as if they had found out about all we know, besides some things that we don't know. Our learned and venerable teacher, of whom we would ever speak with affection and esteem, has shown us in all our paces—trotting through our declamations and reading lessons, at a lively rate—tripping lightly among the big words in the dictionary—limping over verbs, and participles, and relatives, and copulatives—stumbling among cubes and roots, and the vulgarest of fractions—and floundering in a sea of forgotten geographical names and latitudes.

BOY.—I say, Johnny, there's one of your paces he didn't put you through to-day—that's the pace you exhibited when he flogged you round the school-room and out of the window, the other day.

SEVERAL BOYS.—Order! order! order!

HEAD.—I will only say to my tow-headed colleague from Misery Swamp, that if his insulting personalities were not entirely out of place on such an occasion as this, I would stop and settle with him on the spot [*shaking his fist.*]

SEVERAL BOYS.—Order! order! order!

ANOTHER BOY.—That's right, Johnny—stand up for your honor! Form a ring, boys, and let 'em fight it out!

BOYS.—Order! Shame! (*with hisses.*)

HEAD.—Some of you called me to order—I should like to know why.

A BOY.—It isn't parliamentary to shake your fist at a fellow.

HEAD.—I don't care for that. We've nothing to do with parliamentary rules, here—we are governed by Congressional usage; and it's Congressional to shake your fists, and use them, too, if you choose. Does anybody deny that?

A BOY.—Enough said—go on with your speech, Johnny.

HEAD.—Well, as I was saying, we have passed through the fiery trial of another examination, and the magnificent series of prizes—the total cost of which to our beloved teacher, as I learn from good authority, could not have been less than one dollar and twenty-five cents—have all been awarded. As is apt to be the case, I believe, on such occasions, some three or four scholars who are supposed to be brighter than their fellows, have carried away all the prizes, leaving absolutely nothing for the great body of the school. Now it has seemed to some of the more philanthropic members of the class that this is hardly fair; and to equalize in some degree this unjust scale of awards, it was suggested that we all unite and purchase an appropriate offering for the *poorest* scholar in the class. Though it was my fortune, or misfortune, whichever you choose to regard it, to take the highest prize offered to this class, consisting of a touching account of a dear little girl who never was naughty, and died young—

A BOY.—O my! Lend it to me, Johnny, wont you?

SEVERAL BOYS.—And me, too! And me, too And me too!

A BOY.—There, John Head! It's too bad to make fun of your prize.

HEAD.—I beg your pardon, I'm not making fun of it. But I wish folks wouldn't interrupt me. You put me out so, that I don't know as I can get through with my speech. As I was saying, although I took the prize myself, I go in for doing justice to all, and am happy to comply with the request, to present this testimonial of respect and affection to our esteemed friend who heads the other end of the class, as an Irishman might say. Brother Joseph Foot, will you please to rise? [*Foot rises, with a broad grin on his face.*]

A BOY.—Brother Foot is on his feet.

HEAD.—My dear sir, you have been selected as the honorable recipient of a testimonial from your classmates, out of respect to the position you occupy, as the lowest round of our literary ladder. Your quick native intelligence probably will not demand that I should attempt to prove that there must be one round in the ladder lower than all the others; and I suppose it is equally evident to your enlightened mind, that if you constitute this round, yourself, the rest of us can be spared for other and higher posts of duty. We should, therefore, and I trust do, feel truly grateful to you for settling down so permanently and contentedly into this important and truly fundamental office, thus relieving us from all anxiety in regard to it. Your position may seem an humble one, but I may say for myself, that I have considerable respect for it. I like to see a person decidedly one thing or another. Let those eat luke-warm porridge who love it—I prefer mine either hot or cold. Moreover, the brighter scholars of the class are indebted to you not a little for their brilliancy, like the stars at night, which owe much of their beauty to the dark background. But the chief comfort and satisfaction of your life must be the thought that many of the greatest men the world has produced have been very dull and stupid boys. It is said that the bright boys of the school and the college are seldom heard from, when they become men. According to this rule, we may confidently hope to hear a tremendous report from yourself, one of these days.

Accept, then, classmate, this slight token of good-will and esteem, from your friends. It is a heart tribute, whose expressiveness and significance will doubtless be appreciated by you. Accept it—and while you indulge the fond consciousness that you have attained to this distinction without resorting to selfish and unworthy means, you may also comfort yourself with the grateful assurance that you have escaped the sting of envy—that inevitable bane of the prize scholar.

[*He uncovers the testimonial, which proves to be a cabbage, and stepping up to* FOOT, *who stands grinning, proffers it to him.*]

BOY.—Why don't you take it, Jo?—it's a big rose.

ANOTHER BOY.—Yes, Jo, take it—he wont charge you anything for it.

FOOT [*taking the cabbage.*] Wall, I guess it's good to b'ile, any heow.

HEAD.—But, my good friend, you do not propose to consign this token of esteem from your classmates to the dinner-pot, as though it were nothing but a common vegetable!

FOOT [*surveying first the cabbage, and then* JOHN'S *head.*] Wall, 'tis 'most too bad to b'ile it—sich a good likeness o' your top-piece. They say all flesh is grass, but I guess some folks' heads don't want much of bein' cabbages, neow that's a fact. [HEAD *walks back to his seat.*] Jest look, neow! it's the very image of his head, behind, isn't it, you?

SEVERAL BOYS.—Good! Good! Ha, ha, ha!

FOOT [*examining the cabbage.*] Wall, this 'ere's a pooty good sort of a cabbage, any heow, and a feller hadn't oughter make fun of it. But if't belongs to the biggest fool in the class, I shall feel as if I was cheatin' you, Johnny, if I keep it.

HEAD.—O, no, Jo, don't be too modest—there's no doubt you have the best claim—the whole class voted it to you.

FOOT.—Wall, s'posin' I ken prove that you're the feller that oughter had it?

HEAD.—You can't do that little thing, Johnny—if you can, I'll eat the cabbage raw.

FOOT.—I don't take no stumps, but if yer want to bet, jest say so. I'll bet this 'ere 'token,' as yer call it, ag'inst a quarter dollar, that you oughter have it.

HEAD.—Agreed. [*Fumbles in his pockets for money.*] Here's the quarter.

FOOT.—So 'tis! Wall, here's the cabbage. Bill, you hold the stakes, will you? [*Bill takes them.*]

A BOY.—You're sold, Johnny, as sure as a gun! He's got it on to you!

HEAD [*scratching his head a moment.*] Why, Jo is going to put down a quarter, too, isn't he?

FOOT.—No, he isn't going to put down a quarter tew, nuther. I said I'd bet this 'ere cabbage ag'inst a quarter— didn't I, boys?

A BOY.—Yes, that is just what he said.

HEAD.—O, I didn't understand it so.

FOOT.—O, wall, you ken back deown if you wanter—I knowed it would be jest so.

HEAD.—But I shan't back down, so go ahead and win the bet, if you can.

FOOT.—Wont you, though? Seems to me I would, if I's in such a fix.

HEAD.—O yes, you want to back out yourself, don't you?

FOOT.—Wall, no, I've gone so far I wont back eout; but I'll tell ye what, Johnny, I don't want to git away your money, so I'll give in han'somely. *The cabbage is yourn!*

[*General laughter and clapping of hands in the class, with cries of* Good! Capital! You've got to eat it raw, Johnny! &c.]

FOOT.—There, now, I'll leave it to all hands if Johnny hadn't oughter have that 'ere cabbage?

ALL.—Yes! yes! To be sure he had! All right! &c.

FOOT.—Then I'll take that 'ere quarter, Bill—I b'lieve I've won my bet!

[*Renewed demonstrations of merriment through the class.*]

HEAD.—But stop, I thought you just backed out from the bet.

FOOT.—Back eout? No such thing—I said I wouldn't back out, any way. I only kinder made you think I'd give in beat, but I won the wager fairly, arter all, didn't I, boys?

SEVERAL BOYS.—Yes! yes! So he did. It's all fair.

FOOT.—Wall, Johnny, if I've won, I expect that 'ere cabbage b'longs to me, tew. But I don't want to be hard on yer; besides, 'twixt you and I and the teown pump, I don't 'prove of bettin', for dad says it's jest about as bad as gamblin'; so s'posin' we jest swap even—I'll keep the quarter, and you may have the cabbage, and eat it raw or b'iled, jest as you please. It's a pooty good price for it, I expect, but what's the use of a feller's tradin', if he can't make something?

HEAD.—Well, Jo, you shan't say I'm such a fool that I don't know when I'm fairly cornered. I'll own up handsomely, that I went to gather wool, and came home shorn; so you may keep the quarter, and I'll take the cabbage. Here, Bill, pass over the property. [*Bill obeys.*] Boys, I'll just say to you, that the next time you want to make a present to the foot of the class, you will have to get somebody else to be your orator. And to you, Jo, I will frankly confess that you have taught me a lesson I shall never forget. I have learned that a boy is not necessarily a fool, because he is at the foot of his class, and that excellent as book learning is, common sense and mother wit are sometimes more than a match for it.

FOOT.—Thank ye, Johnny; you done that han'somely, that's a fact. Neow, Jake, you jest run over to the bake-shop, and git as much gingerbread as this 'ere quarter will buy, and we'll have a gineral treat all reound. [*Hands him the money.*]

[*Exit* JAKE. *Curtain falls.*]

CHAPTER XIX.

CLOSE OF THE TERM.

"WHAT is the matter, Oscar? you look quite sober," said Mrs. Page, one afternoon, as Oscar came into the kitchen, on his return from school, and began to take off his boots.

"I should like to know," replied Oscar, "why I don't get a letter from home. I've been to the post office every day for a fortnight, expecting one, and it hasn't come yet."

"Why, it doesn't seem a great while since you had a letter from your mother; how long is it?" inquired his aunt.

"Let me see," replied Oscar, reckoning the time in his head; "why, it was just six weeks last Saturday."

"That isn't a very long time to wait for a letter, for a boy of your age, who has been away from home as much as you have," replied Mrs. Page.

"I know it," replied Oscar; "but they agreed to write, some of them, every month; and besides, I believe I think more of letters from home than I used to."

"That is a good sign, if you do," replied Mrs. Page; "only you must be sure and do your share of the correspondence."

"I have done my share," continued Oscar. "I have written regularly every month, almost from the time I came here."

"Then I think you will hear from home soon," replied Mrs. Page.

"Sooner than he expects, perhaps," said a voice from the sitting-room, the door of which, opening from the kitchen, stood ajar.

"Why, mother! is that you?" cried Oscar, springing to the door; "and you, too, father! Why, who would have thought you were in here, hearing me scold about you!"

It was even so. Oscar's parents had arrived late in the afternoon, quite unexpectedly, to make a short visit, and his aunt, as he entered the room, conceived the idea of withholding the news from him for a few moments, to render his surprise the more complete. The warm greeting need not be described; but it may be well to add, that both his father and mother protested that they were not in the slightest degree displeased with the "scolding" they had overheard, and promised there should be no further occasion for it, if they could help it.

The examination and exhibition of the academy took place, in a few days, and a part of the exercises were attended by Oscar's parents. Two days were devoted to this business, and, as usual, they were arduous and anxious days to both teachers and students. The committee who conducted the examination, like the similar body mentioned in the dialogue, seemed bound to find out all that the students knew, and a good deal more. The scholars, however, stood their ground well, and when the examination was concluded, Mr. Merrill, the village clergyman, pronounced it one of the most satisfactory he had ever attended in that place. Then came the closing entertainment, or exhibition, in which speaking, reading compositions, singing, etc., were the order of the day. This, too, passed off quite successfully. The whole concluded with the award of prizes. Among the successful competitors were Jessie Hapley, who took one of the highest premiums, for superior scholarship and good conduct; Oscar, who received a handsome volume, for faithful endeavors; Harrison Clark, who was awarded a prize for general improvement; and Charles Wilder, who received a gift for several fine drawings exhibited by him.

In the evening after the exhibition, all of the students and teachers of the academy assembled at the house of Mr. Upton, the preceptor, to make him a surprise visit. The affair was so well managed, that he knew nothing of the intentions of his pupils until they began to pour into his house. But cheerful fires were soon blazing on the hearths of the principal rooms, fresh lamps were lit, and a dozen or two of chairs were brought in from a neighbor's, which were all the preparations deemed necessary for the occasion. The hours were enlivened with social intercourse, and games, and music, and mirth, in which all participated with the utmost freedom and good-will. No refreshments except apples were offered, one of the elder pupils having considerately informed Mr. Upton at the outset that "they had eaten their suppers once, and considered that sufficient, whether at home or abroad."

In the course of the evening, by some manœuvre which he did not clearly understand, Mr. Upton found himself suddenly surrounded by the whole body of his pupils, and immediately one of their number, a young lady, commenced addressing him in a set speech. She held in her hand an elegantly bound book, which, after a neat address, she handed to the preceptor. This book was entitled, *"The Highburg Academy Offering to their Beloved Friend and Preceptor, Robert Upton, A. M."* It contained the autograph signature of every scholar connected with the institution, to each of which was prefixed a verse or two of appropriate poetry, or a few prose sentences, original or selected, transcribed by the several writers. The volume also contained quite a number of drawings, water-color paintings, maps, etc., executed by the scholars.

The origin of this unique volume was as follows: At the close of several of the previous terms, Mr. Upton had received gifts from his scholars, which were of considerable value in themselves. Fearing the practice of making such presents might entail too heavy a tax on some of the poorer scholars, or subject them to the unpleasant duty of declining to contribute their portion to the fund, he determined to discourage the custom in future. Accordingly a few weeks before the present term closed, he confidentially intimated his feelings to several of the older and more influential pupils, and requested them, in case a presentation should be proposed, to nip the enterprise in the bud. When, therefore, one and another began to speak of presenting a testimonial to the preceptor, they were apprized that such a proceeding would be contrary to his wishes. But this only set their wits to work, and in a little time a project was on foot, which, it was thought, would at once give suitable expression to the feelings of the scholars, and yet avoid the objection he had named to such gifts. A quantity of paper, of uniform size and quality, was distributed among the pupils, and each was requested to write something upon a sheet, and sign his name to it. Drawings and paintings on paper were also solicited, from all who received instructions in those branches, and such as were deemed worthy, were accepted for the collection. These materials were then collected and arranged, and sent to a book-binder in another town, who bound them together into a handsome volume, with gilt cover and edges. Thus, at a trifling expense, a novel, beautiful, and, to the teacher, a really valuable keepsake was procured.

Mr. Upton was quite taken by surprise by the gift, and in his reply to the presentation address, said it was peculiarly acceptable and pleasing to him, because its cost to the donors had been chiefly an expenditure of time, care, ingenuity, and taste, rather than money. A gift procured at such a price, he said, was far more appropriate as an expression of esteem and affection, under the circumstances, than one purchased simply by money, no matter how costly. It was far more precious to him, too, as it contained something which would cause him to remember every one of them, as long as he lived.

As soon as these ceremonies were concluded, one of the boys brought and laid upon the table a portable rosewood writing-desk, of plain but neat and substantial workmanship.

"Mr. Page, will you please to step this way?" said Harrison Clark, who stood near the table.

Marcus came forward, whereupon Harrison proceeded at once to address him, as follows:—

> "DEAR TEACHER:—It is my pleasing task to present to you this writing-desk, in behalf of the pupils of Highburg Academy, and to ask your acceptance of the same. The same

considerations which governed us in the selection of a testimonial for our worthy preceptor, restrained us from procuring a more expensive one for yourself. It is a plain and simple article of utility that we offer you; but though its intrinsic worth be small, we trust it will possess some slight value in your eyes, as a memento of the affection, esteem and gratitude which we all entertain towards you. The ability and success with which you discharged the arduous duties of the preceptor for several weeks, during his illness, the fidelity with which you have labored through the term in your own sphere, the gentle and patient spirit with which you have borne the many short-comings and provocations of those of us who have been more immediately under your charge, and the firm yet always kind manner in which you have led us on in our studies, and restrained us in our errors, have made an impression on our hearts which time will not efface. Many of us hope for a continuance of this pleasant intercourse, in months to come; but those of our number who now meet you for the last time as your scholars, could not let this opportunity pass without a public expression of our gratitude and esteem. Accept, then, dear sir, this slight token of our affection and good will, and may the good Father of all grant you a long, a useful and a happy life!"

To this Marcus responded:

"MY YOUNG FRIENDS:—I came here to help you surprise your worthy preceptor, and had no idea that any such trick as this was in the programme. You have taken me by surprise, most completely. I rather feel as if you had got the advantage of me, too. You knew you couldn't do this to the general, with impunity, and so you thought you would try it on his aid-de-camp. I shall look out for you, another time, you sly rogues! But I wont scold you very hard, this time. No, I will rather frankly confess that this is the proudest moment of my life. Young and inexperienced as I am, such a gift from my first scholars, accompanied by such kind and flattering words, may well make me proud. I accept it with gratitude, only wishing that my poor efforts were more worthy of such a reward. I am sure that no honors or gifts that may fall to my lot hereafter, can ever displace from my heart the memory of this token of esteem from the first pupils I have had the honor and pleasure to instruct. May Heaven reward you for your kindness, and bless you in all your ways!"

The desk presented to Marcus was supplied with a variety of stationery, and was really a beautiful and appropriate gift. He learned, afterward, that Harrison, the once mischievous and troublesome scholar, had been foremost in procuring the testimonial. Marcus always wondered, however, how the matter could have been kept from him so completely, inasmuch as every one in the family but himself was let into the secret.

Oscar's parents were much pleased with the part he sustained in the examination and exhibition, and with the general improvement visible in his conduct, habits and character. They left for home, the next day, but not until they had expressed their warmest thanks for the interest manifested by Marcus and his mother and aunt in Oscar, and their gratification on beholding the improvement he had made under their care. After their departure, Oscar discovered an addition to the inscription in his prize book, written in the delicate hand of his mother. The inscription now read as follows, the first three lines being from the pen of Mr. Upton, and the other three by Mrs. Preston:

Highburgh Academy, Feb. 18, 185-.

———————

AWARDED TO OSCAR PRESTON,

For Faithful Endeavors:

THE FOUNDATION OF ALL EXCELLENCE,

AND THE PLEDGE OF

FUTURE HONOR AND USEFULNESS.

VALUABLE WORKS FOR THE YOUNG.

YOUNG AMERICANS ABROAD; or, Vacation in Europe: the Results of a Tour through Great Britain, France, Holland, Belgium, Germany, and Switzerland. By JOHN OVERTON CHOULES, D. D., and his PUPILS. With Elegant Illustrations. 16mo, cloth, 75 cts.

A highly entertaining work, embracing more real information, such as every one wishes to know about Europe, than any other book of travels ever published.

Three intelligent lads, who knew how to use their eyes, accompanied their tutor on a European tour; and, from a carefully-kept journal, they wrote out, in a series of letters to a favorite companion in study, at home, their impressions of the most remarkable places *en route*. The pencillings are genuine and unaffected, and in all respects form an interesting and instructive record of travel.—*Sartain's Magazine.*

One of the most instructive and delightful books of the age.—*Southern Lit. Gaz.*

Boys, here is a book that will suit you exactly. It is a series of letters from certain boys travelling in Europe to their classmates in this country. It will improve your knowledge and amuse you during long winter nights.—*Methodist Prot.*

It is worth much more than many a larger and more pretentious volume for giving a daguerreotype of things abroad.—*Congregationalist.*

A beautiful book for young people, unlike any thing we have ever seen.—*Ch. Ob.*

Most interesting book that can be put into the hands of the young.—*Olive Branch.*

The best book of foreign travel for youth to be found in the whole range of American literature.—*Buffalo Morning Express.*

THE ISLAND HOME; or, the Young Castaways. By CHRISTOPHER ROMAUNT, ESQ. With Elegant Illustrations. 75 cts.

The best and prettiest book for boys that we have lately seen.—*Boston Post.*

A stirring and unique work. It will interest the *juvenile men* vastly.—*Olive Br.*

Delightful narrative of the adventures of six boys who put to sea in an open boat, and were drifted to a desert island, where they lived in the manner of Robinson Crusoe.—*N. Y. Com.*

A book of great interest, and one which will be a treat to any boy. *Harte Circle.*

The young will pore over its pages with almost enchanted interest.—*Transcript.*

A modern Robinson Crusoe story, without the dreary solitude of that famous hero. It will amuse and instruct the young in no ordinary degree.—*Southern Lit. Gazette.*

A story that bids fair to rival the far-famed Robinson Crusoe. We become as much interested in the fate of Max, Johnny, Arthur, and the rest of the goodly company, as in the Swiss Family Robinson.—*Sartain's Magazine.*

THE AMERICAN STATESMAN; or, Illustrations of the Life and Character of DANIEL WEBSTER, for the Entertainment and Instruction of American Youth. By the REV. JOSEPH BANVARD, author of "Plymouth and the Pilgrims," "Novelties of the New World," "Romance of American History," etc. With elegant Illustrations. 75c.

☞ A work of great interest, presenting a sketch of the most striking and important events which occurred in the history of the distinguished statesman, Daniel Webster, avoiding entirely all points of a *political* character; holding up to view, for the admiration and emulation of American youth, only his commendable traits of character. It is just such a work as every American patriot would wish his children to read and reflect upon.

VALUABLE WORKS FOR THE YOUNG.

BY REV. HARVEY NEWCOMB.

HOW TO BE A MAN; a Book for Boys, containing Useful Hints on the Formation of Character. Cloth, gilt, 50 cts.

"My design in writing has been to contribute something towards forming the character of those who are to be our future electors, legislators, governors, judges, ministers, lawyers, and physicians,—after the best model. It is intended for boys—or, if you please, for *young* gentlemen, in early youth."— *Preface.*

"How to be a Man" is an inimitable little volume. We desire that it be widely circulated. It should be put into the hands of every youth in the land.—*Tenn. Bap.*

HOW TO BE A LADY; a Book for Girls, containing Useful Hints on the Formation of Character. Cloth, gilt, 50 cts.

"Having daughters of his own, and having been many years employed in writing for the young, he hopes to offer some good advice, in an entertaining way, for girls or misses, between the ages of eight and fifteen. His object is, to assist them in forming their characters upon the best model; that they may become well-bred, intelligent, refined, and good; and then they will be real *ladies*, in the highest sense."—*Preface.*

Parents will consult the interests of their daughters, for time and eternity, in making them acquainted with this attractive and most useful volume.—*N. Y. Evangelist.*

The following Notices apply to both the above Volumes.

It would be better for the next generation if every youth would "read, learn, and inwardly digest" the contents of these volumes.—*N. Y. Commercial.*

These volumes contain much matter which is truly valuable.—*Mer. Journal.*

They contain wise and important counsels and cautions, adapted to the young, and made entertaining by the interesting style and illustrations of the author. They are fine mirrors, in which are reflected the prominent lineaments of the *Christian young gentleman and young lady.* Elegant presents for the young.—*American Pulpit.*

Newcomb's books are excellent. We are pleased to commend them.—*N. Y. Obs.*

They are books well calculated to do good.—*Phil. Ch. Chronicle.*

Common-sense, practical hints on the formation of character and habits, and are adapted to the improvement of youth.—*Mothers' Journal.*

ANECDOTES FOR BOYS; Entertaining Anecdotes and Narratives, illustrative of Principles and Character. 18mo, gilt, 42 cts.

ANECDOTES FOR GIRLS; Entertaining Anecdotes and Narratives, illustrative of Principles and Character. 18mo, gilt, 42 cts.

Interesting and Instructive, without being fictitious. The anecdotes are many, short, and spirited, with a moral drawn from each, adapted to every age, condition, and duty of life. We commend them to families and schools.—*Albany Spectator.*

Works of great value, for a truth or principle is sooner instilled into the youthful heart by an anecdote, than in any other way. They are well selected.—*Ev'g Gaz.*

Nothing has a greater interest for a youthful mind than a well-told story, and no medium of conveying moral instructions so attractive or so successful. The influence is far more powerful when the child is assured that they are *true.* We cannot too strongly recommend them to parents.—*Western Continent, Baltimore.*